THE WILD MAN OF THE WOODS

a Story of the Island of Sumatra

MORE WILDSIDE CLASSICS

THE WILD MAN OF THE WOODS

a Story of the Island of Sumatra

ÉLIE BERTHET

WILDSIDE PRESS

THE WILD MAN OF THE WOODS

This edition published in 2007 by Wildside Press, LLC.
www.wildsidepress.com

CHAPTER I

The scene of our story is laid in Sumatra, the great Malaysian island, which is separated by the Straits of Malacca from the most southerly point of India beyond the Ganges.

Even in the present day Sumatra, for whose commerce the English and Dutch so long disputed, is little known to Europeans. Except certain ports at which vessels that coast along the shores of the Archipelago touch, it is rarely visited by travellers. The interior of the country, besides being protected by high volcanic mountains and impenetrable forests, is inhabited by savage, warlike nations, jealous of their independence, and who, though not much addicted to cannibalism, most assuredly would not have the least scruple in devouring any tourists who might be desirous of studying their manners and customs. Therefore, except a few intrepid Englishmen who were not to be daunted by such a risk, no one has succeeded in penetrating into the central regions of the island, and they will remain unexplored till the Dutch, who proceed in this part of the world, as they do everywhere else, with the prudence and gravity of their national character, have contrived to render these people, who now resist every advance of civilization, a little more tractable.

Yet Sumatra would seem, at first sight, to offer the attraction of grand and picturesque scenery, and to possess natural riches which might excite the wonder of the traveller or the avidity of the trader. It is nearly 1050 miles long and 165 miles broad. In this immense territory almost all the productions of the most favoured countries in the world may be met with. The sea that surrounds it is beautiful and calm during the greater part of the year, and numerous rivers, flowing down from the interior, form excellent harbours at many different points. Although the equinoctial line divides Sumatra almost in half, the climate is temperate on the mountains in the centre of the island. These mountains, several of which are active volcanoes, contain precious metals, principally gold, which is worked in a very imperfect way by the Malays. Large lakes supply inexhaustible streams of fresh and pure water.

In the forests the most valuable trees for dyeing and cabinet-work abound. Around the houses fine rice plantations produce the best rice in the world; in every direction there are fields of indigo, pepper, and sugar, and luxuriant plantations, where the clove-tree, the cinnamon, the camphor-tree, the benzoin, seem to rival the cocoanut, the guava, the banana, the orange, and the shaddock, in productiveness and beauty. During six months of the year not a drop of rain falls, the sun shines constantly in an azure sky. Thus, at first sight, life appears pleasant and agreeable in this fruitful land, with its thick, shady foliage and sweet-smelling trees and flowers.

Unfortunately there is a dark side to every picture; in Sumatra, as is often the case, each apparent advantage conceals a deadly danger. The sea, usually so calm and alluring, is subject to typhoons, which agitate it to its very depths. Even in calm weather the European navigator is liable to be surprised at night by Malay pirates, who attack him in their long, narrow, one-decked boats, called flying proas, and murder the" crew and take possession of the cargo. And, when there are no pirates, there are formidable bands of no less audacious sharks wandering incessantly around the vessel. The island itself pays very dearly for its picturesque beauty and fertility. The volcanoes frequently cause terrible earthquakes, which overturn the most substantial buildings. The pleasant rivers are haunted by monstrous crocodiles, ready to snap up the unwary traveller. The virgin forests abound with wild buffaloes, elephants, tigers, and other monsters more terrible still. A thousand dangerous reptiles—among others, the python and the venomous cobra—glide along in the plantations, while the very dwellings are invaded by clouds of insects, which, in tropical climates, seem created expressly to torment the human race. Moreover, the immense masses of decaying vegetation in the marshes and woods emit miasmas, which, in spite of the perfume of the flowers and spice-trees, poison the atmosphere. The length of human life therefore at Sumatra seldom exceeds sixty years, and the western coast of the island is particularly dreaded by vessels in port, and has received from the sailors the ill-omened name of the plague-coast, from its deadly ravages among the crews.

It is, however, on this western coast that Bencoolen and Padang, the two principal settlements of Europeans in Sumatra, are situated; and here too lies the little station where the events of this story occurred.

The place of which we speak was, at the commencement of this century, a little Dutch colony of slight importance. New Drontheim, as this colony was called, was only a trading settlement, to which a few Batavian ships came at certain seasons to seek the productions of the country. It consisted of a harbour, small, but deep and very safe, formed by a river, and sheltered from the waves of the open sea by a little island of coral.

At the mouth of the river there was a fort, armed with certain rusty cannon. Some fifty men, half Dutch, half natives of Java, sufficed for the defence of this post.

Under the shelter of this semblance of a fort, which crowns the summit of the cliff, stretches the village of New Drontheim. The word village, however, must not lead us to picture to ourselves one of our own villages, with houses standing in groups and lying thickly around the parish-church. The houses of this village were detached, according to the custom of the country, and so carefully sheltered by large trees that they were not visible from a distance. Some, of brick, were built in the Chinese fashion; others, apparently only huts of bamboo or cane, were raised from the ground on wooden posts. All the rooms were on the ground-floor, as the earthquakes would overthrow higher and more solid buildings in a minute.

The population of this village, thus scattered over a large space, was composed of almost as many different races as there were houses.

In the first place, a pretty house, half-wood, half-brick, situated in the midst of an evergreen wood, at a little distance from the shore, bore the grand name of the Governor's Palace; it was there, in fact, that the Dutch officer in command of the garrison usually resided, rather than at an unhealthy and uncomfortable dwelling provided for him in the fort at the top of the cliff. The soldiers, following the example of their chief, installed themselves in the village, and lived there when they were not on duty, as was frequently the case; for, except five or six of them who mounted guard by turns in the battery, they had little to do at New Drontheim.

After the Dutch came the Batavians from Java, a set of half-civilized people, who united the vices of the European to those of the savage; then the industrious Chinese, engaged in cultivating the surrounding land; and, lastly, the Malays of different tribes, who lived by hunting and fishing.

The white colonists were less numerous; they consisted of a few English, French, and Portuguese sailors, deserters for the most part, who had provided themselves with families by marrying the yellow, copper-coloured, or black women of the country. In spite of the great variety of races, manners, and languages, the inhabitants of New Drontheim lived very peaceably, and these very different nationalities blended well together; although now and then a few blows with a kris, or knife, were bestowed in private quarrels, nobody taking much notice of the matter.

At the furthest extremity of the colony, that is to say, two or three miles from the fort, was a solitary dwelling, larger and more splendid than the rest, the wonder of the country. It was built on a kind of terrace, half-way up an eminence, forming part of the chain of volcanic mountains which extend over the island. Thanks to this situation, it had little to fear from the pestilential mist which rises every morning near the sea in Sumatra—a mist which for hours resists the powerful action of the sun, and seems to be the principal cause of the unhealthiness of the island. The whole of the terrace was taken up with the buildings, courts, and gardens of the farm. Where it was not protected by inaccessible rocks, it was surrounded by strong palings of iron-wood, rendered impenetrable by hedges of aloes and other prickly shrubs.

The path up to it lay through an avenue of tamarinds, whose thick and majestic foliage furnished the shade so necessary under that fiery sky. At the foot of the hill lay extensive rice-grounds, well-cultivated fields, and magnificent plantations, which apparently belonged to the house. Facing the avenue was the master's dwelling, an elegant Chinese building. Contrary to the usual custom, this house had one story above the ground-floor; but as it was of wood, covered only with that wonderful stucco in imitation of marble of which the Chinese have the secret, it had not much to fear from subterranean convulsions. Beautiful cocoanut-trees raised their leafy fans over its roof, and a veranda or outside gallery, adorned with flowers and climbing plants, stretched along the front. From the top of this veranda, not only the servants and the work-people in the court and in the neighbouring fields might be watched, but an extensive view enjoyed of the valley, bounded by a virgin forest, of the river, of the mountains of the interior, the village of New Drontheim, the fort, the anchorage, and of the vast tracts of the ocean, whose blue waters blended with the sky in the distance.

The head of the family then in possession of this domain was a European, still young, tall, well made, and robust, with a mind apparently as cultivated as his countenance was fine and prepossessing. His name was Richard Palmer; he was of French extraction, and had left Pondicherry and settled in the colony to repair his fortune, which had suffered through the capture of that town by the English.

His wife, Elizabeth, was English. She had fair hair, a pink complexion, and the slender form of the daughters of Albion; and to these decided indications of a Saxon origin she added the languishing sweetness of the Creole. She was hardly eight-and-twenty, and in all the brilliancy of her beauty. From the dignity of her bearing, and the refinement of her conversation, anyone might see that she had been born for society; she still preserved an air of distinction—a drawing-room queen exiled to a savage desert. But if the homage of refined society was no longer hers, Elizabeth did not seem to regret it, and was completely absorbed in her duties as a wife and mother.

Her son Edward, a fine boy of eight, and her husband, whom she adored, took the place of all she had lost. She never complained of the change in her lot; far otherwise, her dear ones always found her ready to welcome them with a smile.

Two other persons, Mrs. Surrey, Palmer's sister, and Anna Surrey, her daughter, completed the settler's family. Mrs. Surrey, it was said, was the widow of an English officer of high rank, who had been killed in a skirmish with the Hindoos. Left alone in the world, with a child of tender years, she had sought the protection of her brother's roof, and both mother and daughter had found in him all the affection they deserved. In the house Mrs. Surrey took upon herself the duties of a good housewife; it was she who directed all the household arrangements, prevented waste, and watched over the general comfort of the family. Her sister-in-law, the graceful and indolent Creole, had long ceased to dispute her position in the family, the duties of which Mrs. Surrey discharged with so much ability.

In return, Elizabeth reserved to herself the care of Edward's and Anna's education. While her husband was directing the work-people out of doors, she, with the help of the few books which formed their library, gave her son and niece the instruction necessary to fit them for civilised life. Anna, two years older than Edward, was gentle, very intelligent, and profited greatly by the instructions of her kind aunt. Edward, on the contrary, made little progress, and greatly vexed his indulgent teacher. He did not like study, and cared for nothing except running about the country, exposed to a thousand dangers, or climbing the rocks, or shooting with a bow and arrows, or following the Chinese or Malay servants about the plantations. It was in vain that Anna, of whom he was very fond, and who had acquired a great influence over him, came to the help of his mother's authority, and tried to make the idle scholar amend his ways; he was always promising to behave better, but it was never long before all his promises were forgotten, and he was indulging again in one of his favourite amusements.

It was now the month of September, near the end of the dry monsoon in Sumatra. And on the day that this story begins, the sky, usually so serene, had been disturbed by thick clouds, and when the sun was setting, dark mists hung over its dazzling disk, though as yet they did not seem to threaten a storm. For all that, the heat was still oppressive, and the inhabitants of our more northern climates would have been overwhelmed by the temperature of a Sumatran autumn.

Mr. Palmer, in a planter's dress, with a large straw hat, jacket, and trousers of nankeen, was standing on the veranda of his house with a telescope in his hand, and observing carefully a little black speck that was just visible on the sea in the distance. At his side, in a large cane chair, was Elizabeth, looking weak and languid. Dressed entirely in white, she was covered with a large gauze veil to keep off the mosquitoes; but this was so transparent that it did not conceal her graceful form, her delicate features, or her eyes so full of love and tenderness when she fixed them on her husband. The temperature was not the only cause of the paleness which marked the beautiful Creole. Mrs. Palmer, like the rest of her family, had been born in India, and had been accustomed to the heat of a tropical country from her birth. But at last the hurtful influence of the climate of the island had affected her frail constitution. Elizabeth frequently suffered from a nervous fever, and the Dutch doctor of New Drontheim had in vain exhausted all the resources of his science in the attempt to subdue it; and at that very time she had hardly recovered from a violent attack that she had had the previous night, although she tried hard to hide her weakness and weariness from her husband.

At the other end of the veranda little Anna Surrey, seated on an easy chair, was holding a lesson-book in her hand. She was dressed in white, like her aunt, and, like her aunt, she wore a gauze veil on account of the mosquitoes. But, throwing aside the troublesome thing, the pretty child left her sunburnt face and neck uncovered, while a light sea-breeze that began to blow played in the silky ringlets of her hair. She was bending over her book, and her lips moved in silence as if she were learning a lesson. Still she seemed in an absent mood, and some secret reason seemed to prevent her from studying with her usual application. From time to time she looked at her aunt, and tried to anticipate every wish of the invalid; but still oftener she looked intently down the avenue which stretched away in front of the house. Evidently she expected someone who did not come, and her uneasiness increased every minute, although she did not dare to express it.

At last Palmer shut up his glass, and said:

"The ship carries the Dutch flag, and has just doubled the point.... No doubt this vessel is one of those that generally come here from Batavia, at this time of the year, to take in a cargo of spices. In less than an hour it will come to anchor, and we shall get some news."

Elizabeth answered with a forced smile:

"Ah, my dear! what do news matter to us now?—we have long ago broken with the rest of the world! Do not think of anything, Richard, but of selling your crops to the captain of the ship just entering the harbour, and do not worry yourself about what may be passing at the other end of the world."

Richard took out his glass again, and began to look out into the distance.

But little Anna could not control her uneasiness; the book she held in her hand was quite forgotten. Thinking the opportunity a favourable one for venturing a question, she glided to Mrs. Palmer, and asked her timidly:

"Dear aunt, where is Cousin Edward?"

"He is gone with the black woman to see the betel gathered," answered Elizabeth absently.

"And are not the betel-fields near the forest?"

"Certainly—but what do you mean?"

"I mean that it will soon be dark, and then—"

A sign from Elizabeth silenced the young girl, as Palmer approached them.

"There, the ship is entering the roads," he said thoughtfully; "and Major Grudmann is sending out his pinnace first, undoubtedly to hail her. . . . Really, my dear, I shall go down to New Drontheim to find out what is happening; I will go first to the doctor to ask him to come and see you, for you do not seem at all well."

Elizabeth did not try to detain him any longer, but contented herself with begging him to return quickly. Richard Palmer was leaving the veranda to start on his walk, when a new incident attracted his attention.

CHAPTER II

Two heavy waggons were entering the court at this moment. These waggons, drawn by black buffaloes, with enormous horns and fierce eyes, were loaded with betel leaf, which had just been gathered. Several men were guiding the intractable team; and at the head of the procession walked, or rather waddled, the China-man Yaw, the manager of the plantations of Mr. Palmer.

Yaw, with his yellow, bloated face, his little slits of eyes, his hanging moustache, his shaven head, and his immensely long tail, which escaped from beneath a hat of rough straw, was exactly like one of those odd figures that everybody has noticed on Chinese porcelain. The only clothes he wore were a pair of drawers and a blue shirt; but the constant grin on his wide face helped not a little to make him look ridiculous in the eyes of Europeans. The char-acter of Yaw was not more attractive than his personal appear-ance. Like the greater number of his countrymen, the manager of the plantations was a coward, a liar, and a cheat; he was grossly avaricious, and would have been rather too fond of opium had it not been so dear.

On the other hand, Yaw was an excellent agriculturist, sober, industrious, always the first at work and the last to leave off; and these qualities, added to his constant gaiety, made his master treat his national failings with indulgence.

Anna no sooner saw him than she called to him, and the Chinaman came, waddling and grinning as usual. Then Miss Surrey, leaning over tile railing of the gallery, and using a kind of *patois* in use among the people of the colony, and composed of all kinds of languages, asked him if he had not seen Edward and the black woman Maria in the plantations.

The fellow nodded his head.

"Yes, yes," he answered; "Yaw has seen Edward and Maria."

"Where were they? where were they going?" asked Anna anx-iously.

"By the forest. Maria not want to go, Edward did want. Edward is small boy, but he be master, and they are gone."

"Into the forest!" cried Anna, clasping her hands; "but has not a tiger been seen prowling about there?"

"Ah, yes! the tiger go about indeed," said the Chinaman, still smiling; "this day, while we worked in the fields, the buffaloes started every minute, as they do when they smell the tiger, and they roared and they looked towards the wood. &ellip; Yaw much afraid, but many buffaloes stronger than one tiger."

The poor child could not control her terror.

"Uncle Palmer! aunt!" she cried; "do you hear? Edward—the tiger!"

But the planter and his wife had not lost a word of this conversation. Richard started up quickly; and Elizabeth, so weak a minute before, sprang trembling from her seat. "My boy! my Edward!" she cried.

"Hush, Elizabeth! hush, Anna!" said Palmer, with authority, although his voice was not so steady as usual; "there's some mistake, no doubt. Let me question the man."

And, addressing himself to the Chinaman in the strange jargon that serves for a common language to the inhabitants of New Drontheim, he asked him some peremptory questions. Yaw replied, still smiling and rocking himself, that about an hour before he had seen Edward and Maria going towards the forest, where signs of a tiger's presence had been noticed during the day.

"Stupid woman!" muttered the planter; "if anything happens to my son, she shall die under the rod."

"Maria did not want to go," answered Yaw; "Edward ran off, and the black woman went after him."

"But you, Yaw—why did you not warn them that it was dangerous just then to go near the forest?"

"Yaw was far off, and he was busy getting in the betel. Work is gold, as the wise man says, and then little Edward is self-willed: he would not have listened to Yaw."

"You should have made them come back. Why did you not go into the wood after him?"

"Oh! oh! oh! the tiger would have eaten Yaw!"

"You stupid coward!" cried Palmer indignantly; "you deserve—"

But casting a look at the foolish countenance of the Chinaman, he remembered whom he was speaking to; and, turning away with an air of disgust, he quitted the veranda.

He went into a room filled with all kinds of weapons, picked out a double-barrelled gun, and slipped a pair of horse-pistols into his belt. As he turned to go out, he perceived that his wife and Anna had followed him.

"Richard, where are you going?" asked Elizabeth.

"To look for this unlucky child; but most likely it is only some fresh frolic of Edward"s: don't be frightened."

"Richard, I will go with you!"

"And I will go, too!" cried little Anna. "I must go and help Edward."

Palmer could not repress a smile.

"What fine helpers you would be!" he said, shrugging his shoulders. "Come, Elizabeth, don't be foolish," he added, in a tone of authority; "I still hope that it will all end with a good scolding to this naughty boy and his rash nurse."

"At least, Richard, have the servants armed, and take them with you."

"Bah! that would be time lost, and then they are such cowards! only one would really be of any use to me, the Malay, Elephant-Slayer. Is he at home now?"

"No, uncle," said Anna, crying; "I saw him go down to the village just now to a cock-fight. And the other Malay, Opium-Smoker, has taken his flock of goats to the mountains."

"Well, then, I shall go alone."

"My dear, dear Richard!"

"My dear uncle!"

Anna and Elizabeth threw their arms round him. He was trying to escape from their embraces, when an inner door opened, and Mrs. Surrey entered hastily. Anna's mother was a lady of about forty, very kind, but as calm and sensible as Elizabeth was nervous and timid.

Palmer said to her quickly:

"You know what has happened, sister; take care of these poor things, and don't let them do anything imprudent; I promise you I will soon bring back the giddy boy who has been the cause of all this commotion. Now, don't let anyone go, I desire."

He darted out of the house, and was soon seen running down the avenue.

Palmer was hardy, expert, and courageous; besides, emergencies of this kind were not very uncommon in his adventurous life. So that, had it not been for his anxiety about Edward, the possibility of having to fight single-handed with a formidable royal tiger would not have troubled him very much. But, even before he reached the end of the avenue, Providence sent him a powerful helper in the person of the Malay, Elephant-Slayer—the very one of all his servants who could render him the greatest assistance. As he was just entering the plantations, he suddenly perceived the Malay returning home, accompanied by his daughter.

Elephant-Slayer belonged to the Batta race, a savage and warlike nation who inhabit the interior of the island, and are even now thought to be cannibals. He was entrusted by Palmer with the care and management of a herd of tame buffaloes; and his daughter superintended the milking. They both lived in a Sumatran hut in the farmyard. However, the duties assigned to Elephant-Slayer by Mr. Palmer were little more than nominal; for the greater part of the time the buffaloes, yoked to wagons or ploughs, were working in the fields, and when they came back in the evening they were taken care of by the other Malay, Opium-Smoker, to whom was also intrusted the care of the goats.

The real employment of Elephant-Slayer was that of hunter for his master's benefit. Armed with a long, heavy gun, he was in the habit of wandering about the surrounding mountains, and sometimes he even penetrated into the neighbouring forest and knocked down wild turkeys, pheasants, and deer, for food for the family. It had thus happened that he had killed several elephants, and, according to the custom of his country, he had added to his Malay name the surname by which he was known.

But he had even killed more tigers than elephants, and these victories had gained him an extraordinary reputation among his countrymen.

Among the Malays of Sumatra the grossest superstitions exist, and one of these superstitions consists in believing that the souls of their deceased ancestors pass into the bodies of tigers and this is why they call these terrible animals *ninis*, or grandfathers. With such a belief, they can have little taste for tiger-hunting, since they may always imagine they see a paternal or maternal ancestor in the ferocious beast they are about to strike. So these men, so brave and ferocious themselves, are rarely disposed to attack the *ninis*. Notwithstanding the ravages committed by these animals, superstition carries the day and they make no resistance. When a tiger enters a village, the inhabitants are even foolish enough to put rice and fruit before their doors, in the hope that these offerings may touch the feelings of their pitiless destroyer.

No Malay would therefore think of hunting a tiger, except in one particular case in which his religion allows it, namely, when a near relation of the hunter has been devoured by a tiger. Now Elephant-Slayer was precisely in this case; his own mother had been devoured by one of these monsters when she had been quietly resting one day before her door.

The fact having been well attested, he might now with a quiet conscience send a ball or a poisoned arrow at all the "grand-papas" that came in his way. Elephant-Slayer was gloomy and unsociable. He was taciturn, false, cruel, and vindictive; he had never been seen to smile, he had never addressed a single affectionate word to anyone. His daughter even did not seem to inspire him with any feeling of love; he treated her rather as a slave than as a beloved child whom he was bound to protect. He found no plea-sure in anything but hunting wild beasts, in quarrels and battles, or else in games of hazard or betting. His great delight was in the cock-fights so dear to all Malays. He trained cocks himself whose sanguinary tempers he was constantly exciting, and he was sel-dom seen without his champion under his arm. Elephant-Slayer had never any pity for his fighting cock except when he gained the victory; then he dressed his wounds and bestowed the most assid-uous care upon him. But, often, if the creature had been cowardly, or had been vanquished, the Malay did not hesitate to strike it with his *kris*, or to torture it with his own hands.

In outward appearance Elephant-Slayer, although full of vig-our, was only of middle height and ill-formed. His complexion was copper-coloured, his forehead low and narrow, he had prom-inent cheek-bones, deeply set yellowish twinkling eyes. His nose was flattened, and from his wide mouth, which displayed teeth blackened and filed to a point, dropped continually that thick, red saliva, caused by the use of the betel nut. His dress consisted of a pair of striped pantaloons, reaching to his knees, and a vest with short sleeves which left his tattooed arms bare. A kind of scarf called a *cayan sarong*, and worn like a Scotch plaid, covered one of his shoulders. For a head-dress he had a coloured handkerchief rolled round his forehead, above which appeared some locks of rough, ragged hair. His legs and feet were naked. Two *krises* with jagged blades hung from his girdle, and completed his rude attire.

His daughter, who walked unnoticed at his side, was slender and well made, and, although her face showed the indelible signs of her race, tolerably pretty. Her dress was not wanting in grace; it consisted of a kind of vest of striped cotton reaching to her hips, and a *bajoos*, or petticoat, fastened round her waist by an embroi-dered girdle; a piece of thin muslin, called *salindag*, served her for a scarf or veil. Her magnificent black hair was fastened in a mass at the back of her head with long tortoise-shell pins, after the Chi-nese fashion. She wore rings of silver on her legs and arms. She excelled in the Echarpe dance, the prettiest dance in her country, and, as a token of her triumphs, they had given her the name of Légère, a name by which she was called both at home and in the colony. The betel-nut, which the Malay women chew as much as the men, had ruined her mouth; but her discoloured, ill-shaped teeth were considered a beauty by her countrywomen; for they are greatly afraid of having white, regular teeth, which they call con-temptuously "dog's teeth." When Palmer met the father and daughter they were returning, as we have said, from a cock-fight, and Elephant-Slayer was carrying his cock all bleeding, and with ruffled and torn feathers, under his arm, but it was doubtless the conqueror, to judge by the caresses that its master was bestowing on it.

The violent emotions that had been awakened in him at the different stages of the struggle had left their traces on his face, for the slightest thing will arouse a storm in men of these fiery natures. At times his eye sparkled with ferocity at the remembrance of some episode in the fight, and a light foam still lingered round the corners of his mouth. However, these impressions were now giving place to an expression of triumph and satisfied eagerness. His daughter went along singing a dance air of a singular character, but not devoid of melody.

At the sight of Palmer the Malay stopped suddenly, not that he intended to show any mark of respect to his master, for that would be contrary to his habits of independence, but he guessed from the planter's look and the weapons he carried that something extraordinary had happened, and he was seized with the violent curiosity peculiar to the savage. Palmer told him in a few words the dangers to which Edward and the black woman were exposed.

This news touched Elephant-Slayer more than could have been expected.

"Edward!—the tiger!" he answered in a hollow voice; "I must get my gun." And he wanted to run home, but Palmer stopped him.

"Your gun?" said the planter; "no, take mine, there is no time to lose; my pistols will do for me."

Elephant-Slayer did not hesitate; he gave the cock to his daughter, bidding her take care of the brave creature; then he seized the gun offered him by Mr. Palmer, and they set off quickly towards the plantations.

As to Légère, after having wrapt the precious bird in the folds of her sarong, she pursued her way home still singing. She had, however, understood very well that her father and her master were going to attack a tiger that had already perhaps devoured Edward and the black woman; but this seemed to her such a trifling matter that she did not think it at all necessary to check the expression of her gaiety.

CHAPTER III

Palmer and the hunter started off through fields of pepper and indigo, and plantations of bread-fruit and cocoanut-trees, striking straight before them that they might reach the forest as quickly as possible. They did not speak, for they were both equally impatient to get there. It was not only a love of fighting and danger that awakened the ardour of Elephant-Slayer; for little as anyone could believe it who knew that iron-hearted man, such a stranger to all tender and natural feelings, he really loved Edward, as much at least as he was capable of loving anyone. It was not the good qualities of the child, his vivacity, his love for his parents and relations, that had touched the heart of the cannibal Batta; such things did not produce the least effect upon him; he would have seen gentle Mrs. Palmer, kind Mrs. Surrey, or the timid little Anna, torn to pieces without being in the least disturbed. What pleased him in his master's son was his faults.

We have said that Edward, though really a good boy at the bottom, was restless, unruly, giddy; that he was fond of any kind of bodily exercise, playing with bows and arrows and other weapons, and he delighted in dangerous adventures. All this charmed Elephant-Slayer; he discovered qualities in this noisy, frolicsome child that he considered likely to make a brave warrior. Besides, Edward, with that natural taste for cruelty that most children possess, and which was encouraged by his manner of life in this wild country, shared his passion for cock-fights, and tried every means in his power to get leave to witness the desperate battles which took place occasionally, when sometimes both of the feathered champions were left dead on the ground. Only a few months before he had made Elephant-Slayer a present of a young cock of a rare kind, which Major Grudmann, the governor of the island, had given him, and this cock had died very bravely on the field of battle. Such a gift had charmed the gloomy Batta more than a handful of Portuguese piastres or Indian rupees, and his affection for his young master had increased in proportion to the bravery of the deceased cock.

Without waiting to stand still, Palmer gave a shout every now and then, but no one answered. It was growing dark, and the silence of night began to prevail. The men were going home from their work, and no doubt the news of the arrival of a ship hastened their return to New Drontheim.

They were now approaching the forest, and its vicinity always seemed particularly dangerous at this time in the evening.

Palmer and the Malay continued to shout at intervals, but they were only answered by the echo; at last, however, as they approached the wood, they had the satisfaction of hearing voices answer theirs.

"There they are," said the planter, gasping for breath; "God be praised, we are in time!"

But this hope was premature; Palmer had not finished speaking when the distant cries assumed a different character, and then they were drowned by a frightful roaring that seemed to make everything around tremble instinctively. Richard and his companion seized their weapons; the planter turned pale, for, above his son's piercing cry for help, he heard the growl of a tiger.

"Let us run," he said.

They rushed forward at their utmost speed; but as they entered the forest they saw the black woman, Maria, running towards them in haste, leading little Edward. Both were shrieking with terror as if they were pursued by an invisible enemy.

At the sight of her master the young and nimble negress, with her clothes all in disorder and her eyes starting out of her head with fright, rushed forward, holding out the child towards Palmer, saying with a broken voice:

"Take him, save him! Little massa no hurt." And, yielding to the violence of her emotions, she fell almost fainting to the ground.

The planter's first idea was to throw himself between his son thus miraculously saved and the part of the wood whence the roaring of the tiger had proceeded; but Elephant-Slayer had already taken this post, and was gazing into the gloomy openings of the forest, where the silence of death now reigned.

Edward, the most charming little rogue you can imagine, was supple, muscular, and tall for his age. Exercise had strengthened his limbs, and the heat of the climate had made him precocious. His open, regular countenance was sunburnt, his eyes were black and his eyebrows strongly marked; had it not been for his fair hair he might have been taken for a beautiful child of the copper-coloured race. His dress was very simple, and consisted of trousers, a short frock of white calico, and a broad-brimmed hat of plaited rushes fastened on his head by a string. Several little arrows with blunt points were stuck in his blue silk belt. Generally his movements were sudden and impetuous, and his way of speaking quick and lively; but now the mischievous child seemed quite scared: either the speed of his flight had made him giddy, or he had really been aware of his danger.

However, the poor father, on finding him again safe and sound, could not contain his joy; he lifted him up in his arms, pressed him to his heart, and kissed him passionately, saying half reproachfully:

"You cruel child, what a fright you have given us! Have you no pity for your mother or me?"

Edward's only answer was a kiss.

But Elephant-Slayer, who had shown so much zeal in coming to the help of his master's son, had turned away from the forest, and, leaning on his gun, was quietly observing this touching scene, though he had not a word, not an affectionate look for this little favourite whom a moment before he had considered lost. He only spat out an enormous piece of betel, and, drawing out his box of *siri*, he took a fresh dose, which he chewed very complacently. Perhaps this was his way of showing his satisfaction, and of congratulating his patrons on the happy result of the adventure.

Palmer, after the first burst of affection, put the child down; and then, looking sternly at the woman seated on the grass, who was hardly beginning to recover her senses,—"Maria," he said, "do you know that you deserve a very severe punishment for this careless conduct?"

"Oh, massa, good massa, not me!—Him—little massa Edward."

And the child hastened to take his nurse's part.

"Papa," he said, very soberly, "do not scold poor Maria, she was not disobedient; scold me, only me. Listen. Mamma said we might go to see the betel gathered; and I went with Maria. I took my bow and arrows to shoot the birds in the rice-fields. But what has become of it? where is my bow?" added the little boy, looking about him uneasily; "I must have let it fall in the wood."

"Never mind," said Palmer impatiently; "we will find it, or you shall have another."

"Oh, but I have never had such a splendid, large bow—Well, then," he added, continuing his tale, "we got to the plantations, Maria and I, and I was looking for birds in the rice-fields when we met the negro Daritis—you know Darius, your valet—and he said to me, 'Massa Edward, have you seen the great flower, down in the wood, at the foot of the old bombax? It is so very big that you might easily lie down inside it.' Then I thought I should like to see the great flower, and I told Maria; but Maria did not want to go, and I ran away. She called me, and I ran away all the faster. I knew where the bombax was, and was determined I would see the great flower. Maria began to run, but I could run faster than she could; I met some of the Chinamen who were going home with the wag-gons, and then I ran away into the forest."

"And did none of those rascals tell you that a tiger had been seen in that part of the wood?"

"Oh! did they know there was a tiger there? I did not know it, and Maria did not. Darius wanted to follow; but Maria was angry, and sent him away. She went into the wood after me, but I hid myself. I was determined to see the great flower, and I was hoping that Maria would get tired of looking for me, and would go away; but she would not go, and kept looking for me and calling me. When she had gone a little way off, I got up and ran to the bombax, and at last I found the great flower. And then I answered Maria, who was crying—she was crying…. O Maria, come and let me kiss you!" added the pretty boy, throwing his arms round her neck; "I am so sorry I vexed you." Palmer listened attentively to this little tale, and seeing that the nurse had not been at all to blame, asked her in a milder tone:

"Maria, is all this quite true?"

The poor negress, who was looking quite delighted with Ed-ward's eloquence, and was listening to him with her mouth wide open, answered, half-laughing, half-crying:

"Massa Edward talk better than Maria, and it all be quite true. But little massa no say anything of tiger yet!"

"Yes, yes," answered the planter, shuddering at the remem-brance; "did not a tiger run after you? I heard him roaring: how did you get away from him?"

"Oh, yes, we did see a tiger," continued Edward carelessly. "We were looking at the beautiful big flower, and all at once we saw a tiger in the brushwood a few steps from us, and he did frighten me, though he was such a pretty creature. Then Maria began to scream, and I cried too, but the tiger cried louder still. He was just going to spring upon us, when a big hairy man, such an ugly fellow, darted forward at the foot of the bombax and hit the tiger with a great stick that he had in his hand. But I did not see the fight, for Maria seized hold of me and dragged me away, running as fast as she could. I dare say I lost my bow there; but I'll find it again." Palmer looked much astonished.

"What does he say?" he asked Maria, "a man bold enough to strike a tiger with a stick! The poor fellow must have been eaten up!"

"No, no, massa; me think the tiger he dead."

"A tiger killed with a stick! it's an absurdity, my poor Maria; and who would be rash enough to do such a mad thing? Did you know him?"

"No, master; but he be very big, very strong. He be one of those men 'who do not talk.' "

Palmer did not understand what she meant, and asked her many more questions; but all he could get from her was that her deliverer was one of those men who cannot or will not speak.

"And he was hideous l" added Edward, by way of commentary.

The planter thought over the story again and again, trying in vain to understand this strange adventure. At length he turned to Elephant-Slayer, who had remained unmoved chewing his betel, and asked him if he were inclined to continue the chase.

"The *nini*'s dead," replied the Malay coolly.

"Dead! How do you know that?"

Then Elephant Slayer explained that the prolonged roaring that they had heard a few moments before had suddenly ceased, which proved that his strength had failed the ferocious beast all at once.

Although Palmer had the greatest confidence in his companion's experience in such matters, he shook his head.

"Well, we must be clear about it," he answered; "for I cannot leave such a brute alive near my house. Elephant-Slayer, we are well armed, and we will go and see if the tiger be really dead. You, Maria," he continued, addressing the woman, "go home quickly with Edward; do not let him get away from you again. Do not stop on the way, for the ladies, particularly my poor wife, must be half dead with fright."

Maria, who adored her mistress, prepared to obey at once, and took Edward's hand to lead him away, but the self-willed little man resisted energetically.

"No, no!" he answered, in a determined tone; "I am with papa now, and there is nothing to be afraid of. I want to see the big flower again, and the hairy man who beat the tiger with his stick—and then I shall find my bow, too. Dear papa, won't you, won't you, dear good papa, let me go with you and my friend Elephant-Slayer?"

Palmer tried to make the wayward child listen to reason; but, as he could not succeed, he consented to keep him, and send Maria home alone. He needed some one to show him the way, and Edward could do that. Then, for fear of accident, he took the little rebel, who would have much rather walked, in his arms, while in his other hand he carried a pistol. Having taken these precautions, he despatched Maria, bidding her tell her mistress that he should be home soon, and then plunged into the forest, followed by Elephant-Slayer.

CHAPTER IV

Although this part of the wood was not very thick, it began to grow dark under the trees, and the most profound silence prevailed.

The least noise, the breaking of a dry branch under the hunters' feet, the flapping of a bird's wing in search of its resting-place for the night, awakened a thousand confused and plaintive echoes. The child pointed out the tree they were in quest of. But he did not chatter as usual; the solemnity of this solitary place seemed to affect even his lively and restless nature.

The ground was uneven and encumbered with the stumps of great trees, which had thrown out vigorous shoots, with cacti and gigantic ferns. Palmer walked slowly, looking carefully at each tuft of grass, and keeping firm hold on his son.

The Malay himself seemed to have comprehended the necessity of being on his guard; he drew the handle of his *kris* from the folds of his dress, and loaded his double-barrelled gun; but, instead of looking carefully on the ground as his master did, he examined the tops of the trees, as if he suspected that some danger might come from them.

They soon found themselves at the foot of the old bombax, where the still unexplained deliverance of the child and the nurse had happened. This tree was one of those gigantic specimens of vegetation, of which nothing that grows in our northerly regions can give us the least idea.

Under its shade grew a plant no less extraordinary, and which might, though for different reasons, have claimed equal attention with it. This was the colossal flower which had excited Edward's curiosity. The Malays call it *krouboul*. It had neither leaves nor stem, and rested on the ground itself; its colour was a reddish white; each of its petals was more than a foot long, and the whole flower was more than ten feet in circumference. It was a giant among flowers, as the bombax was a giant among trees. Unfortunately, this splendid corolla had a very disagreeable odour; God, while He gave it grandeur and beauty, seems to have kept sweet perfumes for less favoured plants.

Edward, at the sight of this botanical phenomenon, found his tongue again, and tried to free himself from his father's hold, to roll himself, perhaps, on the white petals of the krouboul, as on a bed of satin. Palmer, on his part, would not have failed, under any other circumstances, to admire this splendid specimen of the Sumatran flora; but he knew that they were in real danger; and, after casting one absent look on the flower, continued to examine the inequalities of the ground near. As to Elephant-Slayer, he did not appear to be uneasy about what he might find at his feet, and scrutinized the branches of the old bombax with minute care, as it rose like a pyramid of verdure above his head.

All at once Palmer uttered a cry of alarm. In a hollow place, between two projecting roots, he perceived an enormous tiger, crouching as if he were about to spring upon them. He pressed his son to his heart, and was on the point of pulling the trigger of his pistol, when the Malay said to him coolly: "Do not take the trouble—I was right. The *nini* is dead!"

He walked up to the tiger, which, certainly, did not stir, and turned it over contemptuously with his foot. It was a monstrous animal, very little resembling the lean, wasted tigers of our menageries; his powerful head, his still glittering eyes, his huge paws and terrible talons, were indeed calculated to inspire terror. His beautiful striped skin, and his gracefully curving tail, stood out well against the rugged surface of the roots; and Edward, whom his father, being now reassured, had set free, was very well pleased to stroke the silky fur with his little hands. The body was still warm, but it did not stir; and, in spite of the tenacious vitality peculiar to the feline race, the animal seemed to have been killed in an instant.

While Palmer was trying to account for this sudden death, the Malay made him place his hand on the tiger's back. They could feel through the skin that the back-bone was completely smashed. Then Elephant-Slayer made him touch the animal's head; the skull-cap, although it was as thick and hard as a slab of marble, had been crushed in such a way that the bone and the brain seemed reduced to mere bloody pulp. Lastly, in order to complete his demonstration, he pointed out to the planter a thick branch, that had been left by the side of the tiger, and must have been the instrument of death. It was a formidable club, broken off from a casuarina or iron-wood tree, and yet it had been broken by the violence of the blow.

Palmer, greatly astonished, and quite unable to reject the evidence, said:

"I shall never believe that a man can have given such blows; no human power could have killed a royal tiger in this way."

"Orang-outang!" answered the Malay laconically.

This word was like a flash of light to the planter. Then he remembered the marvellous tales that were told of the incredible power, agility, and intelligence of the great apes called orang-outangs by the Malays. He understood at last what Maria had meant by declaring that the tiger had been killed by "one of the men who do not talk;" for, with the negroes, as well as with the Malays, the chimpanzees of Senegal and the orangs of Borneo and Sumatra are only idle men, who have run away into the woods that they may not be made to work. Although Palmer had often heard that there were orangs in the country, it was the first time that any of them had been seen so near New Drontheim.

"What!" exclaimed Palmer, astounded; "I owe my son's life to an orang-outang?"

"An orang-outang!" cried Edward, in his turn. "How I should like to see it! I had no time to look at it, Maria dragged me away so quickly. He is ugly, but he is not wicked, for he killed the tiger that was just going to eat us. I must see the orang-outang."

But Palmer now understood why the Malay had looked at the trees so constantly, and there was reason to think that the conqueror of the tiger was not far away. Night was coming on, the wood was already dark, and the orang is never more formidable than when he is invisible; at the most unexpected moment the hunter drops with a broken head, without having even suspected that the sturdy enemy that has struck him was near. Palmer remembered all this, and his anxiety for his child was again aroused. Taking him up in his arms again, he said, in a stifled voice:

"Poor child! you do not know what you ask. If the stories they tell are true, you need never want to see the horrid creature near."

"What, papa! is it really an animal?" asked the child innocently. "Maria is always talking about these orangs, and she says—"

"Humph!" said the Malay, behind them.

Palmer turned round quickly. Elephant-Slayer pointed with his finger to an object at a considerable height on the old bombax.

"There! there!" he said, in a low voice; "do you see it?" But neither father nor son had sufficiently practised sight to be able to distinguish anything at that height. The perfect labyrinth of leaves and branches on the colossal tree bewildered them, and they could not follow the line pointed out by the Malay. At length, however, there was a sudden movement in the leaves, and a kind of dull sound, issuing from the same spot, served as a guide to them.

At the point where two great branches separated appeared a savage, bearded face with piercing eyes, for there was still light enough in the sky to render it distinctly visible. Its body was concealed; nothing but that broad, impassive countenance could be seen, following with its eyes every movement of the persons below, and seeming to threaten or defy them. Elephant-Slayer raised his gun to his shoulder; but Palmer instantly struck it down, saying authoritatively:

"Don't shoot; I forbid you. However dangerous the orang may be, it has saved my son's life and Maria's: I will not allow the least harm to be done to him."

"And I too, and I too!" cried Edward, clapping his hands; "I will not hear of anybody hurting *my* orang-outang!"

Perhaps the orders of father and son would have availed little had the indomitable Malay quite made up his mind for the attack. At first he did feel angry and inclined to rebel when his master turned aside his gun; but he restrained himself and answered:

"I did not mean to shoot, but only to frighten the orang. He is too high up, and this gun is too small. I shall fetch my own gun, and my lance, and poisoned arrows."

"I forbid you," said Palmer vehemently. "Remember, Elephant-Slayer, if you do any harm now or by-and-bye to this ape that has rendered me so great a service, I shall know how to punish you."

The Malay was incapable of appreciating the generous sentiments of his master; but he made no reply.

In a few minutes Palmer added:

"There is nothing more to be done here; let us go home as fast as we can. I shall not be easy till Edward is out of reach of the orang. Mind, Slayer, listen to me; do not provoke him; it would be dangerous to attack him."

Possibly the hunter shared this opinion, though the danger of the enterprise was its great attraction in his eyes. Palmer continued:

"The tiger belongs to you; you can come and fetch it tomorrow morning with one of your comrades; and I dare say Doctor Van Stetten, who is interested in natural history, will give you more than one gold rupee for the skin."

The thought of this present had a great effect on the Malay, and changed the course of his ideas. Slayer tried to lift the enormous creature on to his shoulders; but he could not succeed. He left it in the place where it was, intending to return for it another time, and then they set off towards home.

Edward, self-willed as usual, tried to resist; he persisted in looking for the bow that he had lost; but already the twilight, always so short in tropical countries, was over, and the stars had begun to shine. Not to mention the proximity of the formidable orang-outang, there was too much danger in such a place to make it prudent to remain longer there, and they gave no heed to the spoilt child.

The creature was still showing his hideous face at the top of the bombax, and, as they walked away, he watched them with fierce curiosity. They had hardly gone twenty paces when they heard a great noise among the leaves, and at the same time a hoarse, guttural, very peculiar cry. They turned round once more: the orang had just raised himself up, and his grotesque form, hanging by one of his long arms from a branch, stood out in black outline against the sky.

A few minutes later and Edward was receiving the caresses of his mother, aunt, and cousin; and, with the artless prattling of a child, was relating to them at great length all that he had seen, done, and said during this eventful evening.

CHAPTER V

Palmer had had too much cause for anxiety to think of the vessel that must have anchored by this time in the river of New Drontheim. But the next morning he remembered his wish to learn the news, and determined to go down to the village, and see what he could hear.

Légère, Elephant-Slayer's daughter, was busy milking the buffalo cows under the posts on which her cabin was built, and she was filling several pans with a rich, sweet milk said to be delicious. The Chinese, under the direction of Yaw, were proceeding in silence towards the rice-fields; while the noisy, chattering negroes were bustling about the sugar and indigo magazines. But the cheerful aspect presented by a farm in Normandy on a fresh autumn morning, when the labourers are starting for their daily work, was wanting.

Neither the yellow, black, or brown men, naked or clothed in strange fashion, nor the barbarous jargon, the strange buildings, the leaden sky, the burning mist hanging over the country, in fact, nothing served to remind a European of the happy scenes of his far distant native land-nothing but the crowing of a few cocks, belonging to Elephant-Slayer, that were celebrating in their fashion the return of a day as stifling as the one before.

After having given orders to some of the servants, and reproved the idleness of others, Palmer was just setting out for the village, when an exclamation in Dutch and a sound of some one panting for breath were heard through the mist, even before the planter could see who was coming. At length the mist cleared away a little, and Palmer found himself face to face with a short, thick man, dressed after the European fashion, who, though it was still so early, seemed to be going to the house.

This individual, a placid, benevolent-looking person, was just then in a great heat, all red and puffy, and panting like a buffalo at bay. He wore a cocked hat, and a faded uniform much too tight for him, while knee-breeches of cloth and coarse woollen stockings completed his dress, which, it must be confessed, was one little suited to the exigencies of a climate like that of Sumatra. The visitor had taken the precaution of carrying his wig, which was powdered with rice-flour, at the end of his umbrella, and yet it was evidently quite time he reached the end of his journey, for he was almost stifled. To add to his misfortunes, the mist, by clinging to the glasses of his great green spectacles, prevented him from seeing where he was, and when he did reach the court-yard, he turned round and round two or three times as if seized with giddiness.

This unlucky visitor was Mynheer Avenarius Van Stetten, Surgeon of the University of Leyden, member of several learned societies, and appointed to superintend the health of the Dutch troops in garrison at New Drontheim.

"Ah! my good doctor," said Palmer, taking Van Stetten's hand to help him; "is it you braving this horrible *cabout*? Don't speak just now, but take my arm. We will go home, and you shall have a glass of French brandy to set you up again."

The doctor tried to answer, but his voice failed, and he allowed himself to be led into a low and, comparatively speaking, cool room. He dropped into a chair, which creaked beneath his enormous weight. However, when Palmer had made him swallow a couple of glasses of excellent cognac, one after another, he began to recover; he drew a long breath, put his wig on his bald head, and having coughed once or twice to clear his throat, said:

"A thousand thanks, Mr. Palmer; you have a famous fog-expeller. Upon my word, I like it as well as our Hollands, which I used to taste now and then at the tavern of the 'Three Kings' when I was a student at Leyden, and we were obliged to work in the anatomical theatre in a cold of ten degrees below freezing point. Ah, who would have thought that I should have missed the ice and snow so much!"

The planter pressed him to take some more; but Van Stetten stopped him.

"No, no," he answered; "have a pity on my poor head. I am not so strong as our old Professor Pomponius, who would toss off a dozen glasses while the clock of St. Peter struck twelve." Doubtless the remembrance of his own country and his young days revived the good doctor, for he did not seem inclined to leave the subject when Palmer asked him:

"You are come to see your patient, are you not, my dear Van Stetten? She is not so well as I could wish; just notice how weak and languid she is, please. As it is still so early, I do not suppose she is up; but I will have her told that you are here—"

He was going to ring the bell, but Van Stetten stopped him.

"Do not wake her," he said hastily; "a quarter of an hour's sleep will do more for our charming invalid than the prescriptions of the whole Faculty. I will see Mrs. Palmer, my dear sir, before I leave the house; but to speak the truth, I should not have been so unwise as to pay you a visit at such an hour if considerations of a pressing nature—"

"Something about natural history, I venture to say," said the planter, smiling; "I could have guessed when I saw Doctor Van Stetten braving the *cabout* that there were plants, insects, or rare quadrupeds in the question."

The good man drew himself up and looked vexed. "That is ingratitude, Mr. Palmer," he replied, "yes, black ingratitude, and you know it well. When I went through the sun, up the mountain that day when you broke your leg in climbing a ravine; when I came here through a frightful monsoon to see Edward when he had had a bad sun-stroke, it was nothing to do with natural history, and I might have expected—"

"I was wrong, Van Stetten, my good friend," interrupted the planter, squeezing the doctor's hand; "you are the best fellow in the world. I was wrong, I say, and I beg your pardon. Well, we will talk of flowers and animals as much as you like; but, first of all, satisfy my curiosity about the ship that anchored in the river yesterday evening. Do you know what she is, and what she is going to do here?"

Van Stetten answered without the slightest temper:

"What! don't you know, Palmer? It is the schooner *Gertrude*, captain Van Roer, from Batavia; he has come here for his cargo of spices. When he goes back I shall send my specimens by him to Batavia, and from there they can be sent to my dear native country. But you will soon see the captain. He seems in a great hurry to lade his ship, and of course he will come first to you, the richest planter in the country, to buy the spices he wants. Now I have answered your questions, let me ask a few in my turn about the escape that my little friend Edward had yesterday."

"Ah, ah! you have heard of his adventure already, doctor," answered the planter; "the news has spread quickly."

"They were talking of nothing else last night in all the huts of New Drontheim; one heard of nothing but tigers, orang-outangs, and wonderful flowers, quite enough to put a humble lover of science like myself on the alert."

Palmer satisfied the doctor's curiosity. When he spoke of the gigantic flower that had attracted the child into the forest, and of the magnificent royal tiger found dead at the foot of the old bombax, Van Stetten manifested his surprise and delight by enthusiastic exclamations. But when Palmer told how an orang-outang had killed the formidable tiger with blows of his club, the savant could no longer contain himself. He sprang from his seat, and, in spite of the heat which made every movement an exertion, he began to stride up and down the room, saying with great animation:

"I have certainly heard of these monstrous apes of the order of *primates* doing extraordinary things, as if they were almost possessed of reasoning powers; but I could never have believed—And one of these singular creatures is in this neighbourhood now? I must see it and study it. How lucky it will be if I am able to discover some new scientific facts about this strange creature and send its skin to Europe, where it is almost unknown. I should present the skin to the museum at Leyden, and it would figure there with this inscription in large letters: *Presented by Dr. Van Stetten, of Leyden.* What an honour and glory! It would immortalise my name. But as you will not let anyone try to kill this orang, I reckon at least on studying it closely; I shall spend my time in that part of the wood where it was seen."

"Take care, my good fellow, that you do not add to the number of the martyrs of science. The forest is very little frequented, as you know, and the animal you want to make observation upon is not the most tractable in the world. People say that an orang, armed with his club, is not afraid of ten strong men, and I can well believe it now, after what I have seen of his doings."

This remark seemed to cool Van Stetten's ardour a little. He sat down again, wiping his face with his handkerchief.

"Really," he replied, "I have heard say that an orang could defend himself even against an elephant. And what is more, he gives such proofs of intelligence that the people of this country look upon him as belonging to a particular race of men who cannot talk. I will take care, as you say, not to add to the number of the victims of science; but I must not delay any longer in going to look at the gigantic flower; as to the tiger—"

"You have no need to disturb yourself about the tiger, doctor," said Palmer, pointing to the window, which was covered with a transparent curtain; "for here it is coming to you."

In fact, Elephant-Slayer and another Malay called Opium-Smoker were entering the court at that moment; they were carrying, suspended from a wooden bar, the body of the ferocious beast, which they had fetched very early in the morning from the forest.

They placed their burden under the shadow of a clump of citron and banana trees; the people of the house ran directly to look at the monster, the hero of all their conversations since the evening before.

A few Chinamen, negroes and negresses, and among others Maria, did not dare to approach, although they knew that the enemy was as dead as a door-nail. The Malays, on the contrary, full of contempt for their cowardice, thrust their naked feet into the tiger's mouth, as if they would like to arouse his ferocity again.

Opium-Smoker, who had been helping Elephant-Slayer, was dressed almost exactly like his companion, except that instead of a handkerchief rolled round his head he wore a queer-shaped hat made of rushes; his face, naturally hideous and ferocious, had that livid, leaden complexion, that besotted stupid look which the habit of smoking opium produces. In truth, all his earnings were spent in buying this fatal drug; and the little peculiar pipe, hanging from his belt near his *kris*, showed that he was always ready to give himself up to his favourite passion. Happily for him, opium was dear and his purse very often empty. If it had not been for this he would have fallen a victim to this wretched mania a long time before, or else he would have had one of those fits of frenzy to which opium-smokers are liable. During these fits they issue from their houses, throw themselves, dagger in hand, on passers-by and kill them, if they are not on their guard; on their part, the passers-by are allowed to attack them and strike them dead like wild beasts. Such was the fate that awaited Opium-Smoker, and the certainty of this inspired the inhabitants of New Drontheim with a horror of him, not unmixed with disgust.

Although the tiger weighed more than three hundred pounds, and the two friends had carried it for two good miles through a hot mist, not a drop of perspiration stood on the bronzed foreheads of these indefatigable men, and they waited quietly in grave silence to be told what they were to do with their prize.

Van Stetten, as you may believe, hastened out, protected from the sun by his enormous umbrella; while Palmer, either more robust or more used to the climate, contented himself with the shade of his large hat made of the bark of a banana tree. As they approached the group collected round the tiger, Edward, still in his morning dress, came out of the house, dragging by the hand his pretty cousin Anna, who tried to resist and turned away her head frightened. The giddy boy ended by leaving her, and after having kissed his father and the doctor, began to play with the tiger's long tail, and almost won a smile from grave Elephant-Slayer. But Anna did not seem reassured by his boldness, and it was only when she had taken refuge behind the negress that she dared to watch the bravery of her valorous cousin.

Van Stetten, sitting down on the ground beside the dead animal, began to examine it with eager curiosity. Palmer took advantage of this to ask the Malays if they had not seen the orang-outang during their morning's walk. Elephant-Slayer indeed had seen it in the thick foliage of the old bombax; but his comrade and he had been too busy in moving the tiger to dream of disturbing the wild man of the woods.

"However," he added coolly, "he seems to have taken up his abode in the neighbourhood of your plantations, and if he is not dislodged pretty speedily he will kill some of your labourers, you may depend upon it."

"Very well," answered Palmer, "we must manage to make him decamp and return whence he came. We will go, a good many together, into the part of the forest where he is and make a great noise; that will be enough, I dare say, to frighten him and make him run away. Meanwhile, I forbid my men to shoot balls, arrows, or darts, at this orang,—you hear me, all of you, don't you?"

At this moment Doctor Van Stetten started up in great consternation.

"Mercy," he cried, "the tiger's bones are smashed; it is impossible to study his anatomy. The skin is all right, however, and a very splendid one; it will make a fine figure among my specimens."

"It is only for you," said Palmer, "to buy it of its owners."

"With the greatest pleasure; what are their terms? Act as our interpreter, Palmer, for I do not understand a word of their abominable lingo."

The planter asked the two Malays what price they put on the tiger. Opium-Smoker's reply was prompt and brief. Elephant-Slayer, chewing his great lump of betel all the time, set forth his claims at much greater length. At last Palmer said in Dutch to the doctor, who was awaiting the result of the negotiation with impatience:

"I knew beforehand what Opium-Smoker would demand. You are a doctor, and your surgery is well furnished with drugs; he asks of you some doses of opium to intoxicate himself."

"He shall have it; but is not the poor fellow stupefied enough already? Does not he know that opium is a poison?"

"He will not listen to reason, any more than the drunkards of other countries, and your sermons would be lost on him. As to Elephant-Slayer, he will not only consent to cede you his share in the tiger, but he will skin the animal very skilfully, on condition—"

He stopped, laughing.

"Go on," said the savant.

The condition is so odd! You will be vexed, perhaps. In fact, he demands that you should bestow your attention on one who is dangerously wounded."

"Dangerously wounded! Is it not my duty to help all who are suffering?"

"Undoubtedly, but this is a peculiar case. In two words, doctor, Elephant-Slayer wishes you to dress the wounds of his favourite cock, a splendid fighting-cock, that received, it seems, a bad wound in yesterday's fight."

Van Stetten gave such a jump, that his heavy green spectacles tumbled over his nose, and his wig turned round on his bald head, casting a cloud of rice-powder all around.

"A plague take him and his cock!" cried he; "does he think that a graduate of the university of Leyden, a licentiate of natural sciences, a doctor of medicine, a corresponding member of the Linnean Society, of the Academy of Berlin, etc., is going to degrade his art by doctoring a spiteful fowl?"

"As there is no university in the forests of Sumatra, I should try in vain, my dear Van Stetten, to make this wretched Malay understand your scruples. As for him, he much prefers his cock to his daughter, and he may think you very much honoured by such a task. Take care; if you refuse his request, he will very likely refuse you his share of the tiger."

"Well, then, if I must give in, I must. I will dress the cock's wound."

The bargain was then concluded, and while the two Malays carried the tiger to a shed near, where they could skin it, Légère, at a sign from her father, fetched the wounded cock.

The doctor was compelled to draw out his case and dress the wounds of the warlike bird, which testified its gratitude by giving him several sharp pecks with his beak.

Then the assembly dispersed; for the sun had got the better of the mist, and its rays, though less unwholesome than the fog of the *cabout*, were really too hot to be borne. The workmen returned to their work, while the members of Palmer's family met in the dining-room for the morning meal. But in vain the master of the house pressed Van Stetten to partake of it; the enthusiastic naturalist obstinately refused, and remained in the shed where Elephant-Slayer, with the skill of a hunter, was proceeding to skin the royal tiger.

CHAPTER VI

In the middle of the village of New Drontheim stood a large shed, used as an assembly-room or *balley* by the inhabitants. Generally to these balleys, which are found in all the little towns of Sumatra, is added a building which serves as a temporary dwelling-place for strangers; but as the colony is surrounded by impenetrable forests and steep mountains, and is only accessible from the sea, it has seemed useless to add this hospitable appendage.

The *balley* of New Drontheim then consisted simply, as we have said, of a kind of shed, with a roof made of palm-leaves, supported on pillars of carved wood. The furniture consisted simply of a few benches.

Now it was usual, when a friendly vessel entered the port, for the people of the place to give an entertainment or *bimbang* to the crew and passengers of this vessel. They were invited to the *balley* in the evening, and there they found all the village assembled to receive them with all due ceremony. Young Malay girls, dressed in their finest attire, paid them compliments, an old man, well skilled in the art of making fine speeches, acting as their mouthpiece; then they presented their boxes of *siri*, or betel, to the travellers, who were bound to take the *siri*, and leave in its place little presents, differing in value according to their generosity. These presents generally consisted of fans, looking-glasses, and other nicknacks from Europe or China. This ceremony performed, the rest of the evening was spent in amusements of various kinds.

It was a fLte of this kind that the inhabitants of New Drontheim gave to the crew of the *Gertrude* two days after the arrival of that vessel; and at the hour appointed for the meeting, the *balley* presented a most animated appearance. Out-of-doors it was one of those warm, clear nights which only occur in the tropics. And the sky was spangled all over with stars. A thousand different kinds of fire-flies darted about in the sky, leaving brilliant lines of light behind them, while, every now and then, the wind brought the sweet perfumes of the clove and cinnamon-trees. A profound quiet reigned around, so that you could even hear the faint, distant murmurs of the forest.

Within, the room was lighted by a great number of Chinese lanterns of coloured paper, such as are now becoming popular in Europe. Hung in festoons, between the pillars which supported the leafy roof, they looked very pretty, and strange insects might be seen darting about around them, splendid moths, attracted by the unusual light. The *kalintangs*, a kind of musical instrument, formed of little gongs, that were struck with a little stick, mingled their sweet and melodious sounds with the voices, male and female, of *improvisatori,* who were holding among themselves one of the musical contests called *jantouns.* In the middle of the room the young Malay girls, in their dresses of embroidered silk, and with rings of gold and silver round their legs and arms, executed graceful dances, waving their scarfs at the same time, while the mothers and duennas, seated, or rather squatted, round the dancers, played the part of wallflowers, as in civilized countries. The rest of the assembly was divided into distinct groups, according to nationalities, colours, costumes, and characters. In the first place, we must mention the Dutch soldiers, proud of their dirty, patched, and scanty uniforms, the original colour of which it was difficult to guess. Gathered together in a corner, they talked phlegmatically of their Dutch canals, on which they used to skate in the winter time, and of their cool little gardens with earthenware statues. Then came the copper-coloured Malays, their heads enveloped in bandannas, who, seated on the ground, were exciting two cocks, whose spurs were armed with steel points, to fight desperately. Behind them were numerous spectators who had bets on one or other of the champions; and at the conclusion of each fight savage cries, curses, and threats were heard, ferocious beyond description. Further in were the opium-smokers, Chinese and Malay, who were giving themselves up much more quietly to their dangerous and irresistible passion. The negroes and negresses met together to laugh and sing, or dance the chika and the bamboula; but all these merry blacks took care to keep out of the way of the Malays, who, on all occasions, showed a profound contempt for them, on account of the whiteness of their teeth. Then there were other motley groups of Hindoos, dressed in calico, Javanese with pointed hats, and some sailors from the *Gertrude,* smeared with tar, and chewing tobacco or betel according to their tastes.

In this numerous, but rather mixed assembly were several persons of our acquaintance. In the first place there was the Governor, honest Major Grudmann, enthroned in a cane chair at the upper end of the room. As a popular sovereign, who wished to show respect to his subjects, he had put on his newest uniform, and his hat with the best gold lace; and he sat smoking his pipe with a dignity more imposing than ever. Behind him stood several persons who formed his suite; namely, three or four inferior officers, and among them Dr. Van Stetten, in his large green spectacles, making observations on the varieties of the human race.

Palmer was there, too, as well as Captain Van Roer, and Mr. Smith. The great lions of the evening were Smith and the captain, who had displayed great generosity towards the ladies and girls of the place; never had *siri* boxes received prettier fans, more magnificent ribbons, or more splendid boxes. This munificence tended to increase the noisy gaiety of the dancers.

Among them Légère, the daughter of Elephant-Slayer, was most admired. Her father remained squatted on the ground among the spectators of the cock-fight. His own cock was wounded, as we know; and, notwithstanding the attention of Van Stetten, the valiant bird was not yet in a state to resume its brilliant career; but Elephant-Slayer betted on other people's cocks, and watched the varying chances of the struggle with extraordinary interest.

At the other end of the balley, in the opium-smokers' corner, was a very different scene.

Among the number of these maniacs it was not surprising to see the comrade of Elephant-Slayer, the taciturn Malay, called Opium-Smoker, *par excellence*. He was able to enjoy himself greatly at this feast, after his fashion, thanks to the rather excessive liberality of the doctor, who had enriched him that morning with a considerable provision of his favourite drug. So he took advantage of the opportunity of getting intoxicated in good company. Stretched on the bare ground, his head resting on a log of wood, he held in his hand the instrument by which he inhaled the vapours of the dangerous narcotic. Seated at his side, Yaw, the head of Palmer's Chinese, helped him with a zeal that could hardly be disinterested, and took good care that the fire in his friend's pipe should never go out.

It may be remembered that Yaw, like the majority of the subjects of the Celestial Empire, had a great passion for opium, and never neglected any opportunity of indulging in this expensive pleasure, gratis. He had the habit, too, when the Malay gave way to a fit of smoking, of coming and sitting down beside him, overwhelming him with caresses, and paying him a thousand little attentions. As a reward for his obsequiousness he was allowed to finish the pipe when the Malay had had enough; not unfrequently, too, profiting by the state of unconsciousness into which his companion fell after a time, he managed to rob him of some grains of opium, which he enjoyed at his leisure.

It was the hope, then, of some such windfall that made him so eager and so attentive. It was a sight worth seeing to watch him, rolling about like a child's tumbler, and grimacing like an idiot, while his long tail wriggled about behind him like an angry snake. As loquacious, insinuating, intriguing, as the other was brutish and cruel, he would say to him in a caressing way:

"Yaw is your friend; friendship is golden. Yaw will watch over you like a mother over her sleeping child. Give yourself up to the delights of this divine gum, and may heaven send you 'vermilion coloured' dreams, dreams full of golden pagodas and sweet-scented tea! Indulge yourself in the ecstasy that makes the poor man equal to the powerful mandarin, that calms the pain of the sufferer, and makes life expand like a flower in the sun!"

These grand speeches, pronounced half in Chinese, half in the *patois* of the country, were lost, no doubt, on the infatuated man, who was becoming already intoxicated; but they lulled him to sleep, as the song of a nurse lulls the infant who cannot understand it. Yaw was not impatient; still smiling and attentive, he kept the pipe alight, taking care that one dose of opium succeeded another, and repeating, as he rocked himself to-and-fro like a figure on springs:

"The man that has a friend is a happy man." While waiting, he gathered up carefully the little bits of the darling drug that were only partly burnt, and watched 'his friend' out of the corner of his slanting eye, that he might know the moment the Malay lost his consciousness; but Opium-Smoker had been long used to opium, and it required a strong dose to intoxicate him. Besides, this nauseous vapour did not produce upon him the quiet ecstasy that the Chinaman reckoned it would; on the contrary, the more he took of the soporific drug, the more his brown face twitched convulsively, the more fixed, and hard, and bloodshot his eyes became.

Still Yaw thought he should soon see sure symptoms that the smoker was completely intoxicated. Then, without interrupting his flatteries, he looked in the Malay's sarong for the box of bark that contained the supply of opium, opened it and filled the pipe again. As his comrade was certainly no longer able to inhale the opium, he stuffed the box into his own dress, and put the pipe to his lips. He did not leave off rocking himself to-and-fro and grinning, and while his long tail swung backwards and forwards with each movement of his shaven head, he repeated, with a well-satisfied air:

"Friendship is golden. It is my turn now! A friend ought to share all he possesses with his friend. I learned that saying from my second cousin, the mandarin of the crystal button, who owns several gardens near Canton."

He began to smoke busily that he might as soon as possible

find himself in the same state as his dear friend, and he did not notice another Chinese at his side, one of those under him, who was watching him that he might play him the same trick when the time came. Neither did Yaw notice that, while he was falling into the much-desired ecstasy without having spent a penny, Opium-Smoker was watching him with a steady, menacing eye, and that the Malay's trembling hand was fumbling for his *kris* in his belt; the pleasure of gratifying his ruling passion having made him forget his usual prudence and cowardice. All at once Smoker uttered a hoarse cry, something like the roaring of a tiger in the forest; and with a frantic effort managed to sit up; his only partial intoxication had allowed him to perceive the abominable breach of confidence of which he was the victim, and a fit of fury over-came the numbness that was creeping over his limbs. He threw himself on Yaw, *kris* in hand; and well was it for the Chinaman that he had not lost his presence of mind and power of motion, or he would never have deceived anyone again. Quick as lightning he sprang on one side, while Opium-Smoker, missing his blow, fell full length on the ground, and buried the blade of his terrible dagger deep in the ground.

All the assembly were alarmed.

"He is *amokspower*" (raving), said one.

"Yes, yes, he is *amokspower*!" was repeated on all sides.

And the women fled instantly; the timid party, that is to say, the negroes and Chinese, prepared to follow their example, while the Dutch soldiers, on the contrary, drew their swords and stood on the defensive.

To understand the full import of the expression, "he is *amoks-power*," it must be remembered that the opium-smokers among the Malays are subject to attacks of frenzy, during which they attack and kill all who approach them, and no one doubted that such was the case with Smoker then. He had attacked Yaw sud-denly, and the rascally Chinese uttered such wild cries as he rolled about on the earth, that everybody thought he had received a mortal wound. They now expected that the maniac would spring up and attack the rest of the unoffending people. And this was why the Dutch soldiers, accustomed to such scenes, drew their swords, while the greater part of the assembly fled in disorder. A ring of naked blades was rapidly formed round the fallen Malay. The Governor had not stirred from his throne, and continued to smoke his pipe with true Dutch composure. When the soldiers turned to him for orders:

"Kill him," he said quietly.

Major Grudmann was, however, an excellent man; but, hardened by the exercise of absolute power in these savage countries, he regarded a Malay intoxicated with opium in the same light as he would a buffalo that had got free, or a venomous serpent.

The soldiers, with the same sang-froid, were going to execute their commander's order, when a man, dashing into the circle, scattered the swords with an incredible disregard of danger. It was Elephant-Slayer who came to the help of his countryman, far less, perhaps, out of affection for him, than out of hatred to the Europeans who were about to strike a Malay.

"Smoker is not *amokspower*," he cried; "but he has been insulted, robbed by that vile Chinese. He was avenging himself, and quite right too. Do not touch him."

He pointed to Yaw, who rose from the ground without any wounds and ran off as fast as his legs would carry him. Opium-Smoker, unable to follow his example, tossed about on the ground, uttering dismal roarings.

The soldiers looked again to Grudmann.

"Well, if he is not dangerous, let him alone," slid the Major, shrugging his shoulders.

The Dutchmen retired unmoved. Elephant-Slayer sat down by his comrade, took away his *kris* by way of precaution, then folding the cloth of his *sarong* round him to make it impossible for him to hurt anybody, he carried him out of the balley.

Five minutes after, the people, finding there was no cause for alarm, resumed the songs, dances, and conversations that had been interrupted.

This incident produced a certain sensation among the Europeans grouped round the Governor. Smith said aloud, with a smile:

"This is a good specimen of the manners of the country! Really, Major, I do not congratulate you on the exquisite civilization of your subjects!"

"Bah, that's nothing!" said the Governor; "things much more serious often happen here, and I require some firmness to maintain order. However, I should have got rid of these two unmanageable Malays long ago; but they belong to Mr. Palmer, and out of consideration for him I have been easy with them and not driven them out of the colony."

"Thank you, sir," replied Palmer; "as for me, I have not yet had sufficient cause to send them away. Generally, Opium-Smoker is only an inoffensive animal, and he does very well to lead the buffaloes to pasture. Elephant-Slayer is considered the best hunter in the colony."

Palmer was anxious to get back to his wife, who was not very well when he left her, and quitted the balley; the Governor went away a little time after, but was soon obliged to return to restore order again. A sailor and a Malay, having quarrelled, had come to blows, and the Malay had drawn his *kris*. The Governor sent him to prison, and peace was restored.

As to Palmer, he went on his way towards home.

The houses in the colony were shaded by large trees, in clusters, forming an unbroken line of foliage to the forest. Under these trees, at this hour of the night, it was perfectly dark, and the darkness was hardly broken at all by the feeble, distant light which proceeded from the dancing-room. However, the planter was advancing without hesitation towards the avenue of tamarind-trees, when a frightful howling, quickly followed by a heavy blow, like that of a hatchet striking the trunk of a tree, was heard at a little distance. Richard stopped instantly.

"What is the matter? who's there?" he asked, in the language common to the inhabitants of the colony.

No one answered; but in a place where the trees were not quite so thick he perceived a man of great stature, standing still with a stick in his hand.

"Who is there?" repeated Richard loudly.

A kind of growl, of a singular character, answered him this time; but the man with the stick disappeared, and all was quiet again.

"Bah!" said Palmer, after waiting a moment; "it is some Chinese, probably in rather a lively state of mind, or some negro intoxicated with cava."

He walked on, and heard nothing more till he reached his house except, now and then, the distant sounds of the Malay flutes and *kalintangs* borne upon the wind.

CHAPTER VII

The garden of Palmer's house was considered one of the curiosities of the colony of New Drontheim.

This garden, as well as the house, was situated, as we have said, at the foot of the great red rocks which enclose that end of the valley. A constant stream of fresh, limpid water flowed down from the mountains. This stream entered the garden close to the orchard, through a double grating in the wall constructed to prevent certain dangerous guests from entering with it. Then, after having filled a pretty basin in which some gold-fish sported, and after winding gracefully among the flower-beds, it left the enclosure at the opposite end, and having watered the rice-fields, flowed into the neighbouring river.

The strange ornaments which the rich Chinaman, who had been the first proprietor, and in fact the maker of the garden, had delighted in scattering about with a profuse hand, were still preserved by its European owner. Winding paths of coloured sand formed a kind of labyrinth, the points of which were marked by little towers hung round with bells, by bamboo bridges, hideous idols, grotesque kiosks, and pagodas. Rare and curious plants grew beneath the shade of magnificent fruit-trees, such as bananas, mango-trees, orange-trees, and shaddocks ; and the same odd taste displayed in the general arrangement of the garden was also visible in the details. Thus a graceful shrub was growing on the back of a porcelain elephant, a charming flower was blooming on the head of a bird, or on the tip of a dog's tail, of the same material.

All the strange figures that we see on lacquered furniture, on Chinese screens and fans, were there in reality. Palmer had not taken the trouble to remove them, and the greater number had fallen into decay. But at suitable places he had made belvederes, which rose above the hedge of prickly shrubs forming a fence round the garden, and from each of these a different, but equally fine view of the plantations, the village, the river, and even of the blue sea bordered by the horizon, could be obtained. The most important of the ornamental buildings with which the garden was adorned, was a pagoda situated near the spot where the stream formed a little waterfall over some rocks; and on account of this situation, it was always cool there in all seasons, which was a great blessing in that hot climate. The way to it from the house was by a path of very thick dwarf trees, through which not a single ray of the sun could penetrate. The pagoda, built half of wood, half of brick, had several pointed roofs, placed one above another, such as one sees on the beautiful porcelain ware of the Celestial Empire. It was painted in brilliant colours, and the front still showed some traces of gilding. The interior consisted of one room, which was rather gloomy, and only furnished with a few cane chairs, a little table, and some mats.

It was here that the morning after the fLte Edward and his cousin Anne had their early breakfast while waiting for the regular family meal. The two children were in the habit of going to the pagoda as soon as they were up, and Mrs. Surrey generally gave them their breakfast. But this morning Mrs. Surrey had been called early into Elizabeth's room, where Richard related to his wife and his sister the events of the evening before. So the negress Maria was told to wait upon the two cousins and to take the entire charge of them; but, tired with having spent nearly the whole night in dancing, she yawned to such a degree that she showed everyone of her thirty-two white teeth, the abomination of the Malays in the neighbourhood.

The breakfast consisted of a large bowl of the yellow, sweet-smelling, creamy milk that the buffalo yields, of bread-fruit and bananas, and cocoanuts freshly opened. The two children, dressed almost alike in white frocks, did justice to the repast with the appetite which is a sure sign of health. They were merry and gay; but Edward was more noisy than usual, because his aunt was away, while little Anna, on the contrary, assumed a dignified and almost maternal air to awe her turbulent companion.

Edward was still on his favourite subject; that is to say, his late adventure with the tiger and orang-outang, and he was declaring proudly that he should go back to the forest soon to see the big flower again, and to look for his bow, a splendid bow that would send long arrows more than a hundred feet. On hearing this boasting, Maria, who had been almost asleep on a chair, started up quickly.

"You not do that, Massa Edward," she said, in a frightened tone; "you not go into the forest, never, never! The man who does not talk would run away with you."

"Run away with me!" answered the child contemptuously. "I should like to see him!"

"God preserve you, Massa Edward," replied the good negress, much agitated; "you too young, not understand. In my country, in Africa, there be these men who do not talk too; but they be black, because there everybody be black, the men that talk as well as the men who do not. Ah, when I was little, they run away with poor negro woman and poor negro boy, and they keep them with them for long time in the woods."

Poor Anna trembled in every limb, but the exploits of the gorillas and chimpanzees of Senegal, which are really said to carry off women and children, made no impression on the self-confident Edward.

"Nonsense! we are not in your country, Maria," he said in his boastful way.

"But the men who do not talk be as wicked in this country as in mine, though they be different colour. Me beg you, dear little massa, not go into the forest."

"I tell you I am not afraid; but tell me, when these wild men of the woods run away with negresses and negro children, do they kill them?"

"No, no, Massa Edward; they give them to eat and to drink, they build them huts; they do them no harm. Black women and black boys come back again some day; but they no more talk; they be savage like them!"

"Oh, you see, they don't do any harm. Besides, this orang is very fond of me; he defended us from the tiger when he was just going to eat us up, so I will go into the forest and fetch my bow."

"Oh, no, no, do not think of it, Edward, dear Edward!" said Anna, in tears, throwing her arms round his neck; "I do beg you—"

The gallant Edward was very much inclined to cry himself; nevertheless, he answered with rather forced stoicism:

"You are a girl, Cousin Anna; but I, I am a man, and I am not frightened like you."

"Well, yes, I am frightened," cried the poor child, almost devouring him with kisses; "do not go—promise me not to go!"

And as the little boy hesitated about giving the desired promise, his cousin, changing her tone, said coquettishly:

"Come, Edward! I see you do not love me!"

"Yes, but I do love you."

"Then you don't want me to love you?"

"I do want you to love me. Are you going to take it into your head not to love me?"

"Do you think I can make myself love you? The next time you bring me flowers I will throw them to the goats, and when you want to kiss me I'll run away—"

For once, the valiant knight was conquered, and began to cry, too; however, he tried one more artifice.

"We shall see then," he replied, in a tone half sad and half threatening; "if you throw my nosegays to the goats, and if you won't kiss me—I am stronger than you, and I'll beat you."

"Very well! I shall cry and let you beat me." Edward could bear no more.

"No, I won't beat you; no, I don't want you to cry!" he burst out. "Cousin Anna, do forgive me, I have been naughty—only forgive me, and I'll do anything you like."

"Then you will not try to go back into the forest, where the horrid big monkey might kill you, or run away with you?"

"No."

"You won't think any more about your bow and the great flower and all the rest?"

"No, no, I promise you."

"Then, kiss me; you shall bring me a nosegay this evening, which I will put in my room to remind me of you, and I will love you always."

So peace was signed and sealed, to the great satisfaction of the negress, who was listening with admiration to the artless prattle of the pretty children. Then she saw them kiss, she clapped her fat black hands, and burst out laughing.

"Well done, well done!" she repeated. "Ah, little miss know how to manage; she will be a clever woman!"

The meal was ended by this time, and Maria set to work to clear it away. The two cousins so lately reconciled seemed to be on the most excellent terms; they vied with each other in trying to efface the remembrance of the quarrel. Anna was not slow in putting Edward's submission to the proof.

"Now, you are a good boy again," she said, timidly and yet coaxingly; "you must not forget that it is time to do your geography lesson. Mamma and Aunt Elizabeth are busy just now, but they will be very vexed if you have not learnt your lesson before siesta."

So saying, the little witch drew out a tattered book which she had hidden in the folds of her white dress. At the sight of this odious old book Edward frowned and began to rebel again.

"Oh, we did not agree to that!" he said gloomily.

But Anna gently persisted; she tried to persuade Edward that he could learn his lesson so beautifully in the pagoda, that nobody would come to disturb him; that a few minutes would be enough for him to do his daily task, and then he would be able to play with a good conscience. At last she succeeded in carrying her point; and, looking very glum, he took up the horrid book.

"If you would only stay with me while I am doing my lesson!"

said the pupil in a piteous tone.

"Oh! I dare say; if I were here you would not look at your book; you would do nothing but laugh and chatter. Now, be brave! If you learn your geography quickly, you will see what I have for you."

"What could the secret be? The pretty child did not know herself; she simply employed a little trick she knew would succeed with her cousin. Once more Edward caught the bait, and opened his book with feverish impatience.

Anna, quite content, gave him a sign of encouragement with her pretty little finger, and went out with the negress, who muttered, smiling:

"Ah, she will be a clever woman!"

CHAPTER VIII

Left alone, Edward's good resolution carried him through at least half his lesson; but as soon as the sound of Anna's footsteps died away, his ardour slackened. He put down his book, then he took it up again, and then he went and lolled on his elbows at a narrow window that looked out upon the garden on the side opposite the house. Without thinking of it he began to watch the beautiful insects that were playing about all around him and humming drowsily, and he became silent and still, as the most noisy children often do when they are left alone.

At this time the fog had not entirely disappeared, but the sun began already to pierce through the yellow mist which settled like gauze round the distant objects, and softened their outlines. Edward had fallen into a very dreamy state, when a certain rustling in a neighbouring ebony-tree suddenly attracted his attention.

The garden, we have said, was surrounded by prickly shrubs, forming an impenetrable wall; but beyond this enclosure was a line of tall trees intended to protect the plantations from the sun; the ebony of which we speak was one of these. Edward could see nothing at first through the dark, thick foliage; but having fixed his attention on one spot with the perseverance of a curious and idle child, he perceived at last an indistinct form in the thickest part. This form did not move, and at first seemed almost a part of the large branch which partly concealed it; but as the mist cleared off, the child distinguished a bearded head, whose sparkling eyes were turned towards him. He could not be mistaken, it was the orang-outang.

On finding himself thus face-to-face with this formidable animal, of which he had heard such extraordinary tales, Edward's first feeling was one of terror, and he withdrew from the window in great haste; but his curiosity soon led him to return to it. There was too great a distance between the ebony-tree and the trees inside the garden for a jump; so that there was no fear of an attack, especially as the window of the pagoda was too narrow to admit the orang. Besides, it must be remembered that Edward felt very grateful to his deliverer, and if he had only that moment promised his cousin not to venture near the forest, it was out of pure condescension. So he soon regained his courage, and examined the terrible visitor with the eagerness of a school-boy who finds an excuse for leaving his lessons for a few moments.

The orang was still partly hidden by the leaves of the tree; but his size was that of a tall man, that is to say, about six feet. His arms and legs were long and thin, though immensely strong; his stomach was large, and his chest square. His whole body was covered with reddish hair; but his face was bare, of a greyish colour, surrounded by a yellowish beard and whiskers. His mouth was wide, and his nose sunken; his little eyes looked gentle enough when he was not angry.

The orang seemed to find as much pleasure in examining Edward as Edward did in examining the orang. Stretched out on his branch, he did not stir, for fear, perhaps, of frightening the little boy away. His countenance was grave and melancholy; he looked in a caressing way at the child.

It did not need much to make Edward believe that he ought to improve his acquaintance with his new friend. He took from the table a bunch of bananas that the negress had left in case he wished to console himself during the fatigues of study by sucking one of these sweet-smelling fruits: he carried it to the window; then, having eaten one banana himself, he threw another to the orang.

The fruit, though thrown with a pretty good aim, would have passed at some distance from the creature, when suddenly a long arm furnished with an enormous hand started out like a steel spring; the banana was dexterously caught in the air, and disappeared immediately into a wide mouth, armed with formidable teeth.

This time the child could hardly restrain a burst of delight; he pulled off the bananas one after another, threw them to his neighbour in the ebony-tree, and had the pleasure of seeing him catch the fruit with the same dexterity. Several of them, however, having been badly aimed, the orang did not try to catch, and did not at all seem to mind losing the delicious prize; one would have thought that he cared less for satisfying his own appetite than for showing goodwill to a weak and pretty creature whom he could have crushed with ease.

This game pleased Edward very much, and, as you may imagine, he quite forgot his lesson. Unhappily, the bananas were coming to an end, and he was thinking how he could get a fresh supply without awakening the suspicions of the people at home, when some loud voices were heard on the other side of the house. The orang became uneasy and crouched down more carefully among the leaves, leaving nothing visible but his eyes, and their expression was gloomy and ferocious. In vain Edward threw him his last banana; the orang no longer showed any wish to catch it; he had decidedly taken alarm, and perhaps from his elevated position he saw something that hindered him from taking any notice of these enticements.

Edward, in his turn, began to listen without further delay. The noise continued to increase, and among the shrill voices of the Chinese and negroes, he recognised his father's deep tones. Judging the opportunity favourable for escaping his geography lesson, he took leave very cavalierly of his friend, quitted the pagoda, and went straight through the house into the court, where a very unexpected sight met his eyes.

The house-servants were crowding thickly round a tree; they were in a state of great agitation, and were making such a noise that it could be heard at the end of the garden. But while the Malays seemed to be giving vent to imprecations and threats, the negroes were uttering lamentations, and the Chinese appeared to be defending themselves with all sorts of gesticulations and ridiculous demonstrations. In the middle of this tumult, Palmer was endeavouring to interpose his authority to obtain a little silence, and Doctor Van Stetten was carefully examining a man stretched motionless on the ground. A few steps behind, the presence of a sergeant and four soldiers in uniform showed that the case was serious enough to require the interference of public authority.

Edward was going to dash through the crowd, when Anna, who was in the veranda with her mother and aunt, called to him in a frightened voice:

"Stop, Cousin Edward; there is a dead man there!"

"Who is it?"

"The Malay Opium-Smoker."

"Yes, yes, come in, my dear," said the two ladies; "such a sight is not fit for you."

But Edward pretended not to hear them, and slipped into the front row of the spectators.

It was indeed Opium-Smoker who was lying there on the grass, with his skull fractured and bleeding. Two blacks going to their work had discovered the lifeless body in the plantations at a little distance from the balley. Their cries had attracted the passers-by; they had placed the corpse on a litter, and had brought it to Palmer's house, to which the deceased belonged.

The child, in spite of his boldness, turned away with horror at the sight, and was perhaps on the point of retracing his steps, when Dr. Van Stetten, who, kneeling with one knee on the ground, had been making a minute examination of the body, got up.

"Gentlemen," he said, "I have formed my opinion; this poor

fellow has been killed by a frightful blow which has fractured his skull, and he has been dead about eight or ten hours."

"I believe you are right, doctor," replied Palmer. "Indeed, everybody could see yesterday at the balley that Smoker was *amokspower*, or on the point of becoming so. No doubt when his comrade carried him out and left him to himself, his head being very much confused with the opium, he fell furiously upon someone passing by, who knocked him down with a stick in self-defence."

"That is what I deny altogether," replied Van Stetten; "in the case you speak of, Palmer, the blow would have struck the front of the head. Now Smoker has been struck from behind; his death is the result of a crime."

The greater number of those present could not understand what was said, as they spoke in Dutch; but one of the negroes belonging to the house said in his jargon:

"It is Yaw, the Chinese, that has killed Smoker, me think. Yaw afraid of him, because Yaw had taken his opium, and Smoker going to revenge himself. Then wicked Chinaman, to be sure, hide himself, and when Smoker went by, he kill him."

"Yes, yes, it is Yaw!" said several voices in different languages.

"The thing is not absolutely impossible," answered Richard; "but how could this cowardly, faint-hearted Chinese dare to commit such a crime at the risk of being discovered? Well! we must question Yaw. Where is he now? In the sugar-cane plantation, I suppose?"

"No, no, massa," replied the negro, who seemed to have a grudge against the Chinaman for some old or recent injury. "Yaw not have been to the fields to-day; he stay at home, not dare to go out. You see very well that he be guilty!"

"Send for him at once," said Palmer authoritatively; "or, stay rather, I will go myself to look for him."

He went towards the frail little building that Yaw occupied in the enclosure; lively discussions were still carried on round the body while the doctor was explaining to Sergeant Muller a point of medical jurisprudence.

Palmer found the Chinese in the greatest terror. Prostrated before a little household god, Yaw was burning pieces of gold paper in order to propitiate the divinity. A man so saving as he was would think twice before offering such a costly sacrifice, but no doubt the danger seemed to him pressing.

At the sight of his master, he got up quickly, and, without waiting to be questioned, broke out with protestations of innocence, accompanied with frantic gestures. He spoke with marvel-lous volubility, using by turns the Chinese language, and all the other languages of which he could remember a word.

"Why are you not at your work?" asked Palmer sternly; "what are you doing here? Why are you frightened if you are innocent?"

"Yaw has a conscience as white as a sheet of paper before the learned man has written on it with his pencil. Yaw was Opium-Smoker's friend-two fingers of one hand. He will give back the box that belonged to Smoker; he never thought of keeping it for himself; he only intended to take care of it for him that he might not get amokspower—"

"That is not the question; I ask you what are you doing here? why do you seem to be hiding yourself when this poor man's death has upset the whole house?"

"Yes, yes! he is dead!" answered Yaw, in grotesque despair. "I have lost the friend of my bosom, the flower of my garden; the lamp of my dwelling is put out. Yaw is afraid of the Malays, who are always trying to plant their *kris* in the breast of a Chinese. Poor Chinaman! always persecuted because misery has compelled him to leave the flowery Celestial Empire!"

Palmer grew impatient with this talk.

"Come," he said, "if you can prove yourself innocent, go and do so before your comrades, and before the armed force that will seize you if you are proved guilty."

Yaw tried to resist; but Palmer seized him with a strong hand, and dragged him into the court, where the supposed murderer was received with cries of indignation and anger. The Chinaman began to defend himself warmly, when all at once his look was arrested, his voice died on his lips; he perceived Elephant-Slayer, the deceased's particular friend, running to the place with all haste. Légère, who was with her father, was speaking to him in a low tone, and no doubt she was relating the tragic event to him, for the Malay wore his most threatening aspect.

However, he did not attack Yaw at once, but leant over the corpse, as if he intended to form his own opinion of the case. In a few minutes, to the great surprise of the spectators, he drew him-self up and said quietly:

"Yaw did not kill Smoker." Everybody exclaimed. The Malay continued, with the" confidence of a man persuaded that he is right:

"Yaw is a miserable Chinese, with no strength or courage; his arm could not have inflicted such a wound. You see, only one blow has been struck, and the skull has been crushed like the tiger's! It is the orang that has killed Smoker."

"The orang!" repeated Edward, as he looked in a frightened way at the trees in the garden.

This assertion was believed by all who were acquainted with the great experience of the Malay hunter; but Palmer, Van Stetten, and Sergeant Muller, who represented at the moment both the civil and military authority, asked for further explanations. Then Elephant-Slayer, with a kind of brutal impatience, explained that the preceding evening, after the scene we have described, he had carried his comrade to the place where his corpse had been found; that no doubt Smoker, struggling against the feeling of intoxication, had had sufficient strength to get up, and that the orang-outang, perhaps attracted into the neighbourhood of the balley by the light and music, had struck him a blow such as no human arm could have given.

This explanation reminded Richard of the cry he had heard as he was returning home, and the gigantic figure, armed with a club, he had seen retreating into the darkness.

"Elephant-Slayer is right," he answered; "what he has guessed, I can almost say I have seen." He related his adventure in a few words, and everybody was soon perfectly convinced of the way by which the herdsman of the farm had come by his death.

Poor Yaw, entirely exculpated, was as extravagant in his expressions of joy as he had been in his grief; it would be in vain for us to attempt to describe his twistings and turnings, his absurd exclamations, his whimsical figures of speech. At last he waddled back to his hut, and, in order to make up for all the troubles of the morning, prepared for himself one of his most delicious dishes—earth-worms cooked in a sauce made of woodlice.

But the fact that Opium-Smoker had been struck dead in the middle of the village made the inhabitants very uneasy, for everybody had good reason to fear a like fate for himself. The invisible enemy would be seizing new victims, no doubt, in the avenues and orchards by day as well as by night, and it would certainly be advisable to rid the colony of such a curse as quickly as possible.

"Me not dare leave my hut to go to the fields," said one of the trembling negroes.

"The orang strikes like a thunderbolt, and his club is as big as the mast of a junk," said one of the Chinamen.

"Well! he does not frighten me!" said Elephant-Slayer, "and I will avenge Smoker's death." "I will not prevent you now, Elephant-Slayer," replied Palmer.

"I intended at first to spare the orang on account of the service he rendered my son, but this last deed of his removes all my scruples. You may set out at once to hunt for this dangerous animal; and any of my men, who would like to go with you, are free to do so, and I will supply arms and ammunition. I should like to have gone myself, but I have sent word to the Governor that I intend to pay my respects to him to-day, and he will be expecting me at the fort."

And he looked at his young wife, who seemed to be waiting for him impatiently in the veranda.

Dr. Van Stetten could not understand this conversation, for it had been carried on in Malay; but Palmer told him the facts of the case.

"That's right, Palmer," he said, very well pleased; "that is a determination that may do something for science. As for me, I will give ten pagodas for the skin of the orang, and then I shall be making a good bargain; for, of all the creatures in the world, there is not one so little known in Europe."

"I will tell our men of your promise, my good Van Stetten, and no doubt it will work wonders. But yet would it not be better to try and take the creature alive?"

"Alive!" repeated Van Stetten; "I would give one of my eyes for a living orang; but who could take him alive, when he springs from tree to tree as if he had wings? Not all the men in the colony would be strong enough to hold him, and he would break every rope like a thread if it were not as strong as a cable. So it would be best to rid the country of him as soon as you can, and let me have his skin to send to the Museum at Leyden as quickly as possible."

The ten golden pagodas promised by Van Stetten to the conqueror of the ape roused the avidity of the spectators, and the hunt was arranged on the spot. Two blacks from the farm, five or six Malays, among whom was Boa, a renowned hunter, and several Dutch soldiers belonging to the garrison, and Sergeant Muller himself, offered to beat the neighbourhood at once under the guidance of Elephant-Slayer, who was appointed leader of the hunt on account of his great experience; Dr. Van Stetten proposing to accompany the expedition as a mere observer.

These arrangements made, Richard ordered the Chinamen to carry the body of Opium-Smoker to the cemetery of the colony, and he sent to the house for arms and ammunition, where a good supply was always kept. When all was ready, someone asked in a determined tone:

"Well, but where is this terrible monkey?"

"Over our heads, perhaps!" answered Elephant-Slayer, looking up into the thick foliage of the trees beneath which they were standing.

The band of hunters were seized with panic at the idea, and more than one had some thought of running away, but seeing their leader remain calm after a rapid examination of the trees, they took courage again.

"He is not there," said Elephant-Slayer; "he must be in some other high tree in the neighbourhood, and we must pay a visit to them all, one after another. He generally lies down on a large branch during the heat of the day. Be on the watch, and on the least movement in the leaves, fire all at once. It takes more than one ball to kill an orang."

Palmer having again advised them to be careful, and to walk close together, they set off, followed closely by the good doctor, whose only weapon was his big umbrella or parasol, for the old thing served both purposes. As for Palmer, after having ordered the negroes who had been left behind to get a palanquin ready to carry Elizabeth to the Fort, he hastened home. Edward had gone to the house before him, and the child was not a little alarmed at the danger which was threatening his friend the orang-outang.

It was plain that the ape, in spite of his prodigious strength and agility, would find himself in a scrape. If he had not quitted his post in the ebony-tree, it would be easy to surround him and cut off his retreat into the woods. However, Edward never thought for a moment of betraying his deliverer's hiding-place; the bleeding form of the Malay inspired him with as much pity as horror, but he resisted these feelings, and obstinately repeated to himself, "Smoker was ugly and wicked—and then the man who does not talk killed the tiger; and I will not have him killed!"

Not being able to resist the temptation of learning what had become of the monkey, he slipped into the garden, and began to watch the great ebony-tree. A slight movement in the leaves showed that the orang was still there. In a little time he saw him even raise his head cautiously, and turn his piercing eyes on the band of hunters. He seemed to be aware of danger, and moved most warily. At the same time he did not appear to mistrust the child; he seemed rather to consider him as an ally, ready to help him in time of need, than as one of his enemy's spies.

Fortunately the hunters, who were examining the trees in the plain, had started in an opposite direction to that of the garden. They were making a great noise, firing every now and then to frighten the orang and make him come out of his retreat. A crowd of colonists, chiefly children, had joined them and were shouting with the same intention. However, it was not likely that the noisy band would think of looking for the enemy so near the houses; they supposed that he would more likely have retreated to the border of the forest, and it was in that direction that they were pursuing their investigations.

Edward's contemplation of the tree was disturbed by some-one calling to him from the house. He must go, and though the danger to his friend was not imminent, Edward could not help saying innocently to him aloud:

"Take care of yourself, poor orang!"

Again the orang showed his intelligent face among the leaves, as if he wanted to thank him for his advice; then Edward, hearing himself called a second time, ran into the house.

Mrs. Palmer and Mrs. Surrey were waiting for him impatiently; his father and mother wished to take him with them to the Fort. He was to go in the palanquin with Elizabeth, who was already dressed for the visit, while his father intended to walk. In a short time Edward was in all the delight of admiring himself in his best clothes, of riding in a palanquin, of not having to repeat a lesson he had not learnt; and the orang, the death of Smoker, and all the events of the morning, were forgotten.

CHAPTER IX

As Mrs. Palmer and Edward reached the residence of the Governor Grudmann, who had seen them from a window on the ground-floor, ran forward to hand out Elizabeth. On account of the heat, the pompous Governor had thrown off his coat and wig, and appeared in a state of undress by no means imposing. Nevertheless, he wished to show the greatest politeness to his visitors; and, as he led them into a room that served for his office, he said to Palmer reproachfully:

"Upon my word, Palmer, this is too bad! You told me you were going to pay me a visit; but you did not say that Mrs. Palmer herself would do me the honour, the pleasure—and you take me by surprise, as you see."

He offered his visitors seats; and Edward, who did not approve of not being noticed, pulled him by the sleeve, and said: "How do you do?"

"Ah! ah! there's my friend Edward!" cried the good Governor, laughing; "I am very glad to see him too. But as for him, I need not thank him for his visit; he would go anywhere, provided he went in a palanquin;" and Grudmann burst out laughing.

The conversation was carried on merrily, for some little time. Palmer cut his visit short, for the weather looked threatening, and he feared a violent storm.

So he and Elizabeth hastened to take leave of the Governor, and, leading Edward away, set out on their return home.

The clouds that had been visible for some days in the usually clear sky of Sumatra now formed a thick veil over the sun, and masses of vapour, rising from the sea, were darkening the air more and more. Still the heat continued overpowering: an indescribable feeling of discomfort oppressed every living thing; nature herself seemed sick, in the anticipation of one of those convulsions so terrible at the equator.

A breeze, as scorching as the air of a furnace, blew only in gusts, and yet the leaves of the clove, coffee, and cinnamon trees fluttered incessantly, while large, lazy waves broke with a loud noise on the shore.

The details of this grand and alarming picture were still more apparent when they left the enclosure of the Fort and reached the drawbridge, from which the sea, the river, and the whole valley as far as the forest, were visible. Looking landwards, the avenues appeared deserted, and the plantations abandoned for the time; for everybody was busy about Van Roer's ship, the *Gertrude*, which was preparing to set sail. The crew were working half-naked, and were trying to complete the cargo, and the negroes and Malays were helping in this hard work; but, overpowered by the extreme heat of the weather, they were all obliged, from time to time, to throw themselves into the river, in spite of the crocodiles, to cool themselves, and get fresh strength and vigour. Yet both land and sea seemed as silent as the grave. Elizabeth had got into her palanquin again, and was trying in vain to obtain a little air by fanning herself with her large Japanese fan. As to Edward, he was allowed to walk home, and running by his father's side, he was looking about him with a childish curiosity that nothing could repress.

As they were descending the winding path that led to the village, the stillness of the plain was broken by a sudden tumult. First the firing of several guns was heard, and then a confused noise of shouting. The sounds did not proceed from the river-side, for the men were going on with their work at the *Gertrude* quietly enough, but from the middle of the village, and it really seemed from Palmer's house.

Richard stopped directly, and ordered the bearers to stop too. It might be dangerous to proceed, and it was only prudent to wait till they could discover what was happening. Elizabeth leaned out of the door of her palanquin to ask anxiously the reason for this halt; but no explanation was necessary.

All at once the shouts and firing began again with renewed vigour, and at a little distance, in the middle of the plantations, a mixed crowd of men and children were seen, running away, as if they were pursued. The author of this sudden alarm was a creature of gigantic stature, whose way of moving about showed wonderful agility. In an instant three or four persons were knocked down, and among the number an individual armed with an extensive umbrella. After this exploit, the conqueror gained a neighbouring palm-tree, mounted quickly to the top, and springing from tree to tree, soon disappeared among the foliage.

"That's the orang-outang!" said Palmer, at last, after anxiously watching the event.

"Poor creature!" cried Edward; "then they have found him?"

But no one noticed the evident regret of the little boy.

"Is it not good Dr. Van Stetten who has been knocked down there?" added Palmer. "Yes, it is, but he is getting up again, I am glad to see, and the others too. Come! they have only been well frightened. The orang had not his club; it was that saved them."

"Thank God!" sighed Elizabeth, falling back on her palanquin cushions; "these orangs are terrible animals."

"Father," said Edward, "as the poor orang has not hurt anybody, will they go after him again? will they kill him? I wish they would not; he saved me,—he is my friend!"

"We must," replied Palmer; "we must get rid of him as soon as possible, or the country will not be safe. Go on," he continued, speaking to the bearers of the palanquin, "there is no danger now."

"Edward, take hold of your father's hand!" said Elizabeth quickly.

They set off again. The shouts and firing still continued, but they seemed to be dying away in the distance. As they reached the village, they met Van Stetten limping along, with his wig all awry, and his clothes torn and dusty. He was proceeding, slowly and painfully, towards his own house.

Mr. and Mrs. Palmer stopped again, to inquire if he was much hurt.

"Ah, my good neighbours," he said, in a tone half-tragic and half-comic, "I shall not forget my meeting with this diabolical ape in a hurry! He is neither a man nor an animal; but a fiend let loose that has iron muscles, and can fly in the air without wings. They dislodged him from the great ebony-tree close to your garden, and chased him from tree to tree as far as your pepper-field, and then, all of a sudden, he fell upon us like a thunderbolt. Without any weapon but his long arms and powerful fists, he knocked down everybody that came in his way, and escaped from us so quickly that no one could say how he did it."

"But are you sure," asked Palmer, "that nobody has been hurt in the skirmish?"

"Elephant-Slayer has had some teeth knocked out in his fall, and his gun has been broken-his old matchlock, you know; Elephant-Slayer will never forgive the orang for this."

"Bah! I will give him another gun. As for his teeth, a Malay's teeth are not worth much." "One negro, I believe, has an arm dislocated; but that I must see to."

"And you yourself, my good doctor," asked Elizabeth, "are not you hurt?"

"Don't speak of it, dear lady. I was thrown down as violently as if I had been struck by the sail of a windmill. My hat was knocked off and my spectacles broken. That I was not killed on the spot, I owe perhaps to my umbrella, which turned the orang's blow aside, and broke my fall. Just see the state it is in."

And he tried in vain to open his umbrella, a shapeless mass of broken wood, bent whalebone and stuff all in shreds.

Richard and Elizabeth could not refrain from smiling; while Edward, in his artless joy, said very quietly:

"Ah! ah! how capitally he has defended himself, my friend the wild man of the woods!" Nobody heard these words. The child asked Van Stetten:

"Doctor, is the orang hurt?"

"No, my boy, none of the balls hit him. His movements are so sudden and rapid, that none of our best marksmen can get a fair shot at him."

CHAPTER X

Several hunters were now seen returning to the village, and speaking in an animated way to those they met, while the noise in the distance did not cease.

"What is the matter now?" asked Palmer; "is the orang coming this way?" Elizabeth started with fright, and Van Stetten prepared to defend himself with his umbrella; but it was a false alarm, and the quiet faces of the village people showed that there was no danger near. A negro from the house, who seemed to be coming from the scene of action, ran to meet his master and mistress.

"Well, Darius," asked Palmer, "what news do you bring?"

"Ah! massa!" answered the negro, with all sorts of strange demonstrations, which might be taken to express joy, or anything else; "him be taken this time!"

"Who is taken?"

"Him—the man who does not speak!"

"What do you say?" cried Van Stetten; "you have succeeded in taking the ape alive? That can't be! He would have beaten you all to powder twenty times over before he would have let anyone of you come near him."

"Ah, massa!" said Darius, still grinning, him be taken, but we not got hold of him yet." "What is this fool of a negro talking about? Tell us what you mean, blockhead!"

Poor Darius, disconcerted by the doctor's roughness, got very confused in his way of explaining himself. Palmer, however, questioned him gently, and was not long in learning the truth.

The ape, having escaped the hunters, went off in a straight line towards the forest, and was not long in getting considerably ahead of them. Unhappily for him there was another open space between the plantations and the great forest, and he found himself under the necessity of coming down to the ground, and walking to reach his usual place of refuge. With the help of a great stick that he broke off a casuarina, or ironwood-tree, he was scrambling across with all possible speed, when he was overtaken by his pursuers. At first he kept them off by brandishing his formidable club; but the balls and arrows were whistling round his head, and, bold as he was, he felt the necessity of getting under shelter as quickly as possible. In his perplexity, he took a step that might have proved fatal to him.

The valley of New Drontheim reaches, as we have said, to the foot of high volcanic mountains, and at the place where the orang was thus pursued some blocks of basalt formed an advanced point on the plain. In the middle of these rocks was a deep cavity, from which flowed a copious stream, and the waters had worn a narrow passage through the rocks which was the only entrance to this enclosed space. Now it was into this passage that the orang was seized with the unlucky idea of entering, hoping perhaps to gain by that means the wooded summit of the rocks; but he was soon undeceived. At the end of the opening he found himself in a deep hole with perpendicular walls, smooth, hard as marble, and which it was quite impossible to climb. He tried at once to turn back, but he was too late. The whole band of hunters rushed upon him, like a pack of baying hounds, at the entrance of the gorge; retreat was impossible.

The orang drew back with a low growl, striking the rocks with his stick, and splashing the water of the stream with his feet. The assailants, on their part, lost no time; some of them kept up a constant shouting to frighten the orang, while the rest rolled great blocks of stone into the opening, only leaving just space enough for the water to flow out. So in a few minutes the formidable animal was shut up in a prison from which neither his extraordinary strength nor his great agility could deliver him.

Such was the event, the news of which the negro had been sent to carry to Mr. Palmer; at the same time he claimed a gun for Elephant-Slayer, who had had his broken in the first struggle. As the headstrong Malay intended to mount guard night and day at the *Fontaine-des-Laves*, as the stream was called, it was necessary for him to be armed, in case, which was not very probable, the orang should try again to force a passage.

Palmer told the negro to follow him home, and he would give him the gun he wanted. As to Dr. Van Stetten, nothing could express his joy when he learned that the orang was caught.

"We shall catch him alive!" he cried. "Darius, you may tell the hunters that instead of ten gold pagodas, I will give them twenty if they bring me this precious animal alive. You may tell Slayer that I will cure his wounded cocks, that I will give him as much opium as he pleases. What a grand thing it will be if I am able to send to Europe the first full-grown orang that has ever been seen there!"

"Take care, doctor," said Richard, shaking his head; "only this morning you thought it would be utterly impossible to secure him."

"But he is a prisoner now; if we do not let him get any sleep or food we shall soon subdue him. I will go and speak to Elephant-Slayer about it at once, and in three days I shall have made him as gentle as a lamb. Want of food and want of sleep succeed with the most ferocious animals."

"What!" said little Edward, with tears in his eyes, "you mean to starve the poor orang, that saved me from the tiger ?" No one answered him.

"Darius," asked Elizabeth, "are you quite sure that the orang cannot escape from the place where you have shut him in?"

"No danger, ma'am; we throwed stones as big as a house into the opening; he no more get away; and the hunters, too, guard the passage carefully. Me have mounted on a rock to look at him at the bottom of the ditch. How funny he do look down there. He grind his teeth and want to tear me to pieces—and me laugh!"

At the same time, Darius showed his white teeth, and clapped his hands with almost childish joy.

"But can't he climb up the sides of the ditch? They say these monkeys climb so well, and are so strong!"

"No danger, I say once more, ma'am," answered the negro; "if you only saw, twenty feet deep! For that the man who cannot talk get out of that, he must have a rope tied to one of the trees at the edge of the pit, and thrown down to him. But who throw the rope? not Darius, very sure!"

"A rope" murmured Edward; "it only needs a rope to save him?"

And he began to think.

"Well, Richard," said Elizabeth to her husband, "as there is nothing to be afraid of, let us go on."

They took leave of the doctor, who returned in all haste to Fontaine-des-Laves; and, accompanied by Darius, they pursued their way home.

Half-an-hour later, Anna and Edward might have been seen in a room on the ground-floor under the care of Maria. The negress was busy making up a dress of a fine deep lemon colour, which, with a poppy-coloured silk handkerchief for a head-dress, would form a toilette, she thought, that would dazzle all the blacks in the neighbourhood at the next bimbang.

But as the poor woman was not a very clever dressmaker, she would have made but poor work of it if Anna had not helped her with her needle and good taste. Thanks to Anna, the dress did seem almost fit for a human creature; and Miss Surrey was making the utmost use of her pretty fingers to finish the work, to the lively satisfaction of her companion.

Edward moved restlessly about the two workers; he was more serious and less noisy than usual, and seemed very busy making himself a new bow. However, he frequently stopped in his work to go to the window overlooking the garden, and gazed at the ebony-tree in which he had seen the monkey that morning.

Once when he turned silent and pensive to his cousin, the latter, without stopping her work for a minute, asked him in an absent manner:

"Edward, have you learned your geography lesson?"

"Of course I have."

"Then say it to me while I am working."

"I have not my book."

"That does not matter, I know it by heart."

"But—but I have forgotten it since the morning."

Anna looked at him reproachfully and sighed.

After a minute's silence, Edward continued:

"Anna, did you hear them say that they were going to starve the poor orang? It must be a horrid thing to be starved!"

"So it must be; the creature saved your life and Maria's, and I cannot help pitying it."

"You do pity it?" asked the child, trembling; "then you would not be sorry if it did escape from Fontaine-des-Laves?"

"I should be very pleased."

Anna, in saying this, was only expressing a feeling of pity, and she little guessed how many tears this unfortunate speech would cost her.

Edward seated himself in a chair more quietly than was at all usual with him. But suddenly he got up again and went to the door.

"Where are you going?" asked his cousin.

"You know very well," answered Edward, somewhat embarrassed, "what you told me this morning. I am going to pick you some flowers."

"Go, if you like. You will find pretty flowers in the garden."

"In the garden!—oh, dear! there are much prettier at the foot of the waterfall."

"I don't want those!" answered the little girl in a peremptory tone; "I will not have them!" "Then I will go into the garden."

"Massa Edward, you no go far," said Maria as he went out; master want to take you to see the sailors go away."

"All right! I will be there."

And he left the room. Anna and the negress continued to cut out and stitch very busily. As the child did not come back, Anna left her work for a minute and went to the window. She saw Edward in the garden, plundering the flower-beds. Reassured, on this point, she went back to her seat, and listened to an interminable story that Maria was telling to keep her patiently at work with the hems and fells of the yellow dress.

More than half-an-hour passed in this way. It was getting dark, the weather was becoming gloomy, and the storm, that had been brewing all the morning, now seemed imminent; Anna stopped the negress in the middle of her story—

"Where can Edward be?" she cried, running again to the window.

She called her cousin. No one answered; but she found on the window-sill a charming bouquet that had been put there for her. She took the flowers, but her anxiety did not decrease, and she said with some agitation:

"Where can he have gone? He is so rash, so venturesome."

"Don't worry, Miss Anna," replied the negress, "but finish the gown very quick for poor Maria. Dare say little Massa Edward gone with massa, whom me heard go out just now."

"That's it," answered Miss Surrey, breathing more freely; "he must have gone out with his father. He might have said good-bye to me."

And she pouted coquettishly; but soon began to smell the bouquet, smiled, and resumed her work. Richard, it was true, had just gone out, but alone, to be present at the departure of the ship. Not wishing to expose his son to the coming storm, he had made up his mind to leave the child at home, and had left the house quietly.

When Palmer, in a great heat, reached the port of New Drontheim, the vessel had already gained the middle of the river. Palmer made his adieux to the captain and his company, who then went off in a boat to the ship.

A few minutes after, Grudmann and Palmer found themselves alone on the shore with a few lookers-on. The ship sailed along with difficulty, being impelled by such an uncertain wind. At the moment it drew near the little island at the mouth of the harbour, a great noise was heard landwards, clouds of sand blew wildly about, the trees groaned and bent to the ground, the river and the sea, which were a dull leaden colour before, were covered in a minute with a foam as white as snow.

When the squall fell on the ship, it bent over in such a way that it looked as, if it must go down; but it rose again directly and advanced towards the open sea.

"What a wind!" said the Governor; the *Gertrude* will make a good, quick passage, I hope."

"Don't you think, Major," asked Palmer anxiously, "that a

tempest that begins in this way may be very dangerous for friends on board?"

"Well, the wind blows from the land, so it is favourable for going out of port. If once the vessel is out of the river, the storm may rage as much as it likes; if it blows a hurricane the *Gertrude* won't mind."

In spite of the Major's confidence the *Gertrude* struggled with difficulty against the storm, whose violence increased every minute.

The ship had taken in almost all her sails, and for a moment she rolled over on her side, beating the waves with her lower yards; but she rose again quickly, and cut a way proudly for herself through the foaming waters. She directed her course towards a kind of little strait that she must cross to gain the open sea; but, before she reached it, the waves became so high, the mist which filled the air so dark, and the clouds of dust so thick, that those on shore lost sight of her completely.

The Major hurried home to avoid the rain that he knew would soon fall in torrents, and of which the distant thunder already gave warning. Palmer remained alone on the beach at the risk of being blown down by the wind, or carried away by one of the monstrous waves that dashed violently on the shore, and tried again and again, but in vain, to get a glimpse of the flying ship on the horizon. A fresh occurrence, however, compelled him to turn his attention to another quarter.

In the midst of this war of the elements, several shots, and then frightful cries at the other end of the settlement, were heard. Richard tried to discover what could be the cause of this noise; but on the land, as well as on the sea, it was impossible to distinguish anything a few steps off, in spite of the dazzling lightning that was beginning to flash. The planter, haunted by a vague presentiment, determined to go to the village to learn what it was. So he set off to walk, but not without difficulty, for the wind threatened every minute to throw him down, and he was blinded by the dust, dry leaves, and rice straws that were flying about all around him. At last he gained a spot a little more sheltered from the tempest, where he met Darius, who was running about like a madman, or as if he were himself the plaything of the furious wind.

Darius had not perceived Palmer when the latter called him. On recognising his master, the negro seemed at first to wish to avoid him; but after a little hesitation he went up to him and said, in a voice that could hardly be heard in the midst of the uproar of nature:

"O master! master! such a trouble! You die of grief!"

"What has happened, Darius?"

"Me not dare say—such a great trouble! Dear little Massa Edward!"

"Edward!" exclaimed the planter; "what do you know about Edward? Speak, speak at once, I tell you!"

The negro was so frightened that his teeth chattered.

"No, no, never!" he cried, "you would kill me. Mercy, mercy, master! poor Darius be innocent of all!"

"I won't hurt you; I only want to know what it is about my child, my Edward. Will you speak, you rascal?"

He tried to seize Darius by the arm; but he sprang back.

"No, no, me cannot tell!" he repeated, almost beside himself go to Fontaine-des-Laves, then you learn the truth."

And he ran off as fast as he could go, leaving Palmer in the greatest anxiety. The planter tried to call him back and to run after him, but Darius was already far away. Palmer then, almost distracted, set off for Fontaine-des-Laves, where he was to learn the explanation of the negro's words.

CHAPTER XI

Let us now return to Edward, who had disappeared in such a singular way while his cousin had thought him busy gathering flowers in the garden.

The thought that they were going to torment the captive ape by depriving him of food and sleep, or even kill him perhaps, worked in young Palmer's brain. After the tales of the negroes and other people about him, Edward no longer looked upon the ape as a beast, but as a kind of man deprived of speech; or, at least, as a being half-way between a man and a brute. So his childish honour led him to think that he ought to pay his debt of gratitude to his deliverer. But how was it to be done? Darius had certainly said that a bit of rope would suffice to work the prisoner's deliverance, but where should he find a rope? And then how should he get out of the house? The first person that met him alone in the country would think it right to take him home, where he would get a sharp scolding for his prank.

Busy with these reflections, which, as one would naturally expect in so young a child, were rather vague, he made up his bouquet, placed it on the window-sill, and slipped into the court. He had no fixed plan yet; he would have obeyed the first call from the house. But his father was writing in the drawing-room, his mother and aunt were up-stairs; Anna was listening in the little room to an African story that the negress was telling; nobody seemed to be thinking about him, and he was left to follow the suggestions of his adventurous disposition.

He walked mechanically towards a building used for storing away the different crops. In the confusion caused by the events of the day, the door of this magazine had been left open, and the child could go in without any difficulty; cords of different sizes were kept there to fasten up packages and bales. Edward took one, and hid it in his dress in a hurry. However, he did not yet know what he meant to use it for, and perhaps thought, at any rate, it would do for a swing or some other childish game.

This little theft committed, he began to wander about the court. It was quite deserted. A Sumatran hut, built on piles, with a wooden ladder up to the door, seemed to be the only one where anybody was at home. A monotonous song, not altogether wanting in melody, issued from it; it was Elephant-Slayer's daughter humming to herself. After a time Légère came down the ladder. Though she was not dressed in all her holiday ornaments, yet she still preserved the proud and rather hard beauty that characterizes the Malay women. Draped in her sarong, she was carrying an earthenware pot on her shoulder, and was supporting it with her bare arm, like a sculptured statue; in her other hand she held something wrapped up in a palm-leaf.

She went on singing, and chewing her betel, and she was going away without paying any attention to Edward; but the child went up to her coaxingly:

"Légère," he said in the patois of the colony, "where are you going?"

"To Fontaine-des-Laves," replied Légère, without looking at him.

"And why are you going to Fontaine-des-Laves?"

"To take my father his food, and to tell him about the wounded cock."

"Is the cock getting well?"

"Yes."

And she was just going on when Edward caught hold of her by the folds of her sarong.

"Légère, listen, do. I love you very much; do take me to Fontaine-des-Laves."

"What do you want to do there?"

"I want to see the orang that they have got prisoner there."

The Malay girl was very much flattered by this request; for in spite of her national pride she had often envied the familiarity that existed between her master's child and the other women belonging to the house. However, she answered dryly:

"You are forbidden to go out with me. My master and mistress will scold me, and my father will beat me. Go home!"

Edward was offended at this not very gentle refusal; but his desire to go to La Fontaine only increased with contradiction, and he answered, coaxingly:

"You know why they won't let me go out with you? It is because they say Malays eat human flesh. Aunt Surrey told me a story of a horrid woman who ate children, and who had pointed teeth like yours. But I am not afraid of being eaten—I am a man; and then the horrid woman was ugly, and you are very pretty."

This artless reply, which seemed, however, so cleverly put in, induced the young girl to consent.

Did Légère want to play a trick on those who accused her of cannibalism, or did she only yield to the irresistible power of flattery? Perhaps both motives influenced her, and she answered: "Come, then."

She set off at a good pace, and, though she was barefooted,

Edward had some difficulty in keeping up with her.

The child was afraid at first of being seen from the house, and while they were in the avenue he kept looking behind him anxiously; but they soon left the beaten path, that they might take the shortest way to Fontaine-des-Laves. Then not being afraid any longer of being met and taken home, Edward was soon at ease again, and recovered his natural assurance.

Légère, as she crossed the fields of rice and pepper with her pot on her shoulder, did not seem to trouble herself about her little companion, and went on humming.

"What are you carrying there, Légère?" asked Edward carelessly.

"Not human flesh, child. It is a piece of goat, and some rice, and bread-fruit cooked in the ashes."

Edward, abashed by this rough reply, did not venture to say any more; and Légère continued her song, taking a bit of betel from her box every now and then.

At the end of a quarter of an hour they reached Fontaine-des-Laves. Elephant-Slayer, Darius, and the other hunters, were guarding the rocks at the source of the stream. Certain that the orang could not climb the walls of the cavern, they contented themselves with guarding the passage by which he had entered, to hinder him, if need were, from throwing down the pieces of rock that closed up his prison. However, they did not really believe such a thing possible, even for their vigorous adversary, for they were fulfilling their task very negligently, and, lying on the grass, they were playing at dice and other games of chance popular in the colony.

The sight of Edward caused them some astonishment and uneasiness. Although there seemed no cause for alarm, they could not see the beloved son of the richest planter in the neighbourhood exposed to one of the accidents so common in that terrible country, without apprehension. Darius wanted to take him home again directly, and tried to take hold of him; but Edward resisted, scratched, and bit so violently, that the poor negro, not daring to employ force, let him go, determining to watch all his movements and prevent him from doing anything he should not. On his part, Elephant-Slayer seemed much irritated with his daughter, who had acted as guide to the child, and he scolded her well in Malay.

She did not put herself out at all.

"He would come," she said coldly, placing her provisions on the ground.

Edward hastened to have his say.

"Yes, I wanted to come," he answered, in a resolute tone; "and who could hinder me? I am master, surely; and I am not afraid." This decision in so young a child could not fail to please Elephant-Slayer.

"And why did you want to come?" he asked Edward more gently.

"To see the wild man of the woods." The Malay pointed with his finger to the blocks of basalt, at the top of which were some trees and brushwood; and anyone looking down from there could see into the pit where the orang was confined.

It would be mere play for Edward, accustomed to all kinds of bodily exercise, to climb the rock; but, before trying the ascent, he seated himself on a stone at Slayer's side, and said to him in an insinuating tone: "Have you not given the wild man of the woods anything to eat since the morning?"

"Nothing."

"Won't you throw him something this evening?"

"No."

"And to-morrow?"

"No. The orang is fierce because he is strong; hunger will subdue him. When he has fasted for three days, he will let himself be taken and bound. Then I shall give him to Van Stetten, who will pay me twenty gold pagodas,—and I shan't let anyone else have any of them!" he added, as if speaking to himself, and putting his hand on the handle of his *kris*.

"But if," asked the little boy, "hunger does not make him more gentle, what will you do?"

"I shall climb the rock, and shoot him with poisoned arrows. They do better than bullets; but they forbid us to use them."

Edward, on learning the fate of his protégé, felt inclined to cry, but he restrained himself.

"O Slayer, you won't be so wicked as to make the poor orang suffer like this? Only think,—he killed the tiger that was going to eat me up."

"Yes; but he killed Smoker, a Malay, and a Batta, and he broke the gun that was my father's. I will be revenged!"

Now Edward burst out crying.

"Slayer," he said, clasping his hands. "let the wild man go, I beg you. When I am a big man, I will give you a great many golden pagodas, and fine guns, and fighting-cocks. But I shall be so sorry if you torment or kill the poor orang that saved my life."

Edward had gone the wrong way to work; tears and supplications produced no effect on the fierce hunter; Elephant-Slayer shrugged his shoulders.

"You are a child," he said contemptuously; "and a Batta warrior should not have listened to you so long."

He turned away his head, and began to eat the provisions that his daughter had brought. Then, having eaten as much as he required, he played away the remains of his meal with the other hunters, who had not left off their games of dice and hucklebones.

Thus Edward was left to his own devices. Darius, who ought to have watched him, was chatting with Légère. No one stirred when the child, after hesitating for some minutes, began to climb the rocks. Scrambling up on his hands and feet, he soon reached the top. There, he found himself on the edge of the chasm, and looked down fearlessly. In spite of the growing darkness a little basin was visible at the bottom of the fissure, from which the clear, limpid water was flowing gently out in the channel which served to carry it away. On a narrow ledge of ground which surrounded the basin was the orang-outang. The walls, being perpendicular, rendered every attempt to escape from this well-like place useless.

The orang had, however, made incredible efforts to climb up, as the state of his nails and his hands, bleeding from the roughness of the rock, testified; but now, leaning against the rock, his long arms hanging down by his side, his eyes sad and gloomy, he stood motionless, and seemed to have lost all strength and courage. Then he heard a slight noise overhead, he started and looked up. No doubt he recognised Edward, for his eye, all at once, assumed an expression so sad, so gentle, and at the same time so supplicating, that it was impossible not to be touched by it.

Up to this time, we repeat, the child had not clearly made up his mind what he meant to do. He had come there as much out of a spirit of opposition and curiosity as with the intention of helping his friend in distress. But seeing the orang so weak, so dejected, almost dying, he felt an ardent desire to help him without delay and by any means.

"Oh, dear! perhaps he is hungry," he thought.

He drew a beautiful ripe fig from his pocket, which he had reserved for his own particular use, and threw it generously to the orang; but the latter seemed too much afflicted by his present situation to dream of eating. The fig fell close to him, and he did not exert his usual skill in catching it; he still continued to gaze at the child with eyes full of intelligence, grief, and entreaty, as if to beg more effectual assistance.

Then Edward remembered the rope he had in his pocket; but,

before putting it to any use, he resolved to see what the hunters intrusted with the blockade of the Fontaine were doing. Elephant-Slayer, with his usual desperation, was playing at dice with his comrades, while Darius and Légère were still chatting. No one was noticing little Palmer; nobody seemed to be thinking of him.

Having made sure of this point, he began to undo the rope he had brought. Although it was pretty thick, yet it seemed much too weak to bear the weight of such a wild, heavy creature. Besides, supposing it did not break, how could the orang, exhausted by fatigue and hunger, raise himself up to the edge of the chasm? And the least noise, the least failure, would attract the attention of the hunters, and render the enterprise altogether impossible. In spite of these apparently insurmountable difficulties, Edward, to quiet his conscience, fastened one end of the cord firmly to the trunk of a palm-tree that had struck its roots into the clefts of the rock; and then he threw the other end into the cavern. He hardly expected any result from such a simple contrivance, but still he leaned over to see what would happen.

What happened took place so rapidly that he was struck dumb with astonishment. The orang had watched with marked attention, but without stirring, all Edward's movements. When he saw the rope drop, weak as he was, he raised himself at once; with one prodigious leap, he sprang across the basin of the spring, seized the rope, and climbed to the top of the rock with inconceivable agility. In the twinkling of an eye he was at his deliverer's side, and, brandishing his club, which he had not thrown away, he uttered a hoarse, commanding shout, as if to proclaim his triumph!

Edward forgot the exchange of good offices that had passed between him and the orang, and was almost frightened out of his senses when he saw this strange, hideous creature, of gigantic stature, spring up before him like an evil spirit let loose. He tried to run away, his limbs failed him; and he fell into the brushwood, uttering cries of terror.

The hunters took alarm immediately, and they had little trouble in guessing part of the truth. Their play and talk were put a stop to, and each one seized his bow or his gun, and began to climb the rock; but, notwithstanding their haste, they came too late.

The orang went up to Edward, picked him up carefully, and was turning him round with an air of surprise when the hunters arrived. Threatened by so many enemies, he settled what to do at once. He threw away his club, pressed Edward to his shaggy breast, and, seizing with his other hand the trunk of the nearest tree, climbed to the top, in spite of his burden, with the rapidity of thought.

The hunters, seeing the only child of the rich planter carried up into the air in this way, trembled lest he should be dropped from that frightful height, and did not dare to use their weapons, for fear of hurting him. As for the child, made giddy at first by the rapid motion, he was not long in coming to himself, and began to cry for help in all the different languages he knew. Then it was that Elephant-Slayer and the rest, in the hope of frightening the orang into leaving his prey, fired a few random shots, and uttered the shouts that were heard far off in the country.

This proceeding did not have the result that they expected. The orang did not intend to give up his prisoner so easily; hugging afresh the poor child, who was still uttering cries and supplications, he sprang lightly to the next tree, and from that to another, till it was soon evident that he would succeed in gaining the forest, where he would be sheltered from all pursuit.

Although these rough men were not easily affected, they did seem touched by the terrible situation of Edward, and left nothing undone to cut off his captor's retreat. They descended the rock, and ran hither and thither, shouting incessantly, and loading and firing their guns. Unfortunately the trees, though sometimes rather scattered, reached without interruption to the forest, and the orang, by springing from one to another, was able to brave their attacks.

Another circumstance now increased the difficulties of the pursuit. The violent wind that preceded the storm had already risen in the valley, as we have said, and was raising clouds of dust and dried leaves, while the trees, beating against one another, made a frightful tumult. In the midst of this commotion, the hunters, blinded and deafened, could no longer follow the movements of the orang or hear the lamentations of his victim.

Besides, Edward's voice grew weaker and weaker, either because he was so high up, or because he was out of breath with the prodigious leaps that the orang made with so much ease and agility.

The last time that they were both seen, they were on the old bombax, at the foot of which the scene with the tiger had taken place a few days before. For a moment there was an interval of calm, and from a distance they could distinguish the great form of the orang-outang and the white clothes of the little boy.

It was strange; but one would have said that the orang was

aware of the suffering and fatigue of the frail creature he had stolen. He took pains to save him from too violent shocks, and very cleverly pushed aside the branches that might have hurt him.

For a minute even, seeing that he was some way in advance of his enemies, he stopped for an instant to let him take breath, and rocked him gently in his long arms like a nurse. In spite of these precautions, Edward seemed nothing but a dead weight; his frail body was bruised as if he had had a violent blow, or as if he were already dead.

But very soon a fresh blast again darkened the air; when it ceased, and when the summit of the bombax was again visible, the orang and the child had disappeared.

The hunters lost all heart; the undaunted Elephant-Slayer alone went on, saying:

"The orang has done me an injury,—a Batta warrior must revenge himself !"

He was very rash to venture into these solitudes so late in the evening, where he would be exposed to all kinds of dangers. Some of Slayer's comrades, however, followed him into that part of the wood where the colonists had made some clearings; but at the border of the forest itself they dispersed under pretext of continuing the search in different directions. In truth, convinced of the uselessness of trying to deprive the orang of his prey, they now only thought of getting shelter from the storm as quickly as possible.

CHAPTER XII

We now know what was the terrible misfortune that Darius told his master had happened. When Palmer, distracted and breathless, reached Fontaine-des-Laves, he found no one there but Légère, who was quietly gathering up the remains of her father's dinner. She was just going away; but Palmer stammered out, in a broken voice:

"Where is the wild man of the woods? Where are they all? What has happened?"

Légère looked at him in an absent way, took a lump of betel from her box, and answered at last without any emotion:

"They have all gone after the orang."

"Tell me," continued the planter, trembling with impatience and fear, "what has happened here just now?"

"The wild man of the woods has run away, and carried off the child."

"What child?"

"Edward,—master's little boy. Edward threw a rope to the orang, and the orang ran away and took Edward with him."

We must pardon Légère for her heartlessness; she was a Malay, and she was not a mother; who could have made her understand that such news, told in such a way, might have been a death-blow to poor Palmer?

On learning the terrible truth, Palmer felt as if a dagger had entered his heart; but he hardened himself against the feeling, and asked, in a voice scarcely intelligible, which way the orang had gone. Légère pointed to the old bombax, and he rushed off in that direction, exclaiming:

"Edward, my darling Edward! what will Elizabeth say?"

The girl watched him as he went, struggling with the violent gusts of wind; then she lifted the pot on her shoulder again and returned home, without seeming to have any idea of the harm she had done.

In a few minutes Palmer reached the bombax; but he looked in vain for his child's captor, or the hunters that had pursued him. It was growing dark rapidly, the fleeting brightness of a few distant flashes of lightning scarcely relieved the increasing darkness. The planter tried to shout, but the roaring of the storm drowned his voice.

Sometimes, in the midst of the uproar, he thought he distinguished sounds of lamentation, and human voices answering to his call; but he soon found that he had been deceived by the kind of dismal groaning that the wind makes as it dies away in the forest.

Nevertheless Palmer was not to be daunted. Unarmed, bareheaded, for he had lost his hat as he ran desperately along, his clothes in rags, his hands and face bleeding with the thorny shrubs through which he dashed, he went on his way at all risks, calling his son with a voice that was hardly audible.

As he was wandering thus in the darkness, a dark form suddenly appeared at his side. He guessed, rather than recognised, that it was Elephant-Slayer.

He asked him quickly if he had any news of his son.

"I have seen nothing," answered Slayer angrily.

"Well, we must go on looking," replied Palmer energetically. "Slayer, you are a brave, experienced hunter; you are acquainted with life in the woods; help me to find my darling Edward."

"To-morrow."

"Why to-morrow? why not this very minute? Perhaps by to-morrow the wretch will have throttled my boy, or else the child will be dead with fatigue and terror."

"The orang will not kill Edward," said the Malay coolly; the men who do not talk are fond of children, and take great care of them. Master, don't go into the forest now."

"Do you think, then," answered Palmer impetuously, "that I am afraid of tigers and other wild beasts? I shall take the child back to his mother, or perish in the attempt!"

"Slayer is not afraid either; but we can see nothing, we can hear nothing, during the night and during the storm."

"It is beginning to lighten, and in a little time the lightnings will make the wood as light as in the day-time; perhaps we shall be able to see my son."

"Master! Master!" answered the Malay impatiently, "don't disturb the orang; he is hiding no doubt somewhere near; if you do disturb him he will certainly run very far away with Edward, and we shall never find them again."

There was some justice in these remarks; but the fatherly affection and blind despair of the planter hindered him from seeing it.

"I won't leave my child like that," said he. "I will never leave these woods till I have found him, even if I have to hunt for him all night."

And he turned to enter the wildest part of the forest, from which just then a frightful noise issued—a sound as if all the wild beasts in the world had met there to howl at once. The Malay, offended at this obstinacy, did not try any more to detain him, and was going to return to the settlement, when someone was heard calling in the distance. At the same time torches were seen among the trees, and several persons appeared, running quickly. As Richard turned round, his wife, pale and tottering, threw herself into his arms, crying in a broken voice:

"Richard! dear Richard! where is our child?" Mrs. Surrey had come with Elizabeth as well as little Anna; all three in the loose dresses they wore in the house, and without anything on their heads. In fact, Légère had not been more careful in telling her mistress how Edward had been carried off than she had been in telling her master. On learning the terrible news, the gentle mother had fainted; but she soon recovered, and, with the strength of fever and despair, set off towards Fontaine-des-Laves. Anna and the quiet Mrs. Surrey, herself hardly less overcome, had followed her, mingling their cries and tears with hers. Everybody belonging to the house, even the most selfish and impassive Chinamen, had accompanied the unhappy family. A few of the villagers had joined them on the way, and they arrived just when Palmer, mad with grief, was trying to penetrate the inextricable thickets of the primeval forest. Elizabeth's question seemed to excite her husband to the last degree.

"I will bring him back to you, Elizabeth," he cried, "I promise you. Leave me alone—go home! I must recover the son that God has given me for my comfort and joy!"

"Ah! is he not my child as well as yours?" answered the mother impetuously. "Richard, I will not leave you !"

"And me too!" cried little Anna, sobbing.

"Oh, do let me go with you to look for Cousin Edward!"

By the light of the resinous wood torches that the negroes carried, Palmer looked at his wife and the child who wanted to be his companions in his perilous expedition. Pale, feeble, and out of breath, they could hardly stand; and it was a wonder how they had managed to come so far. While he was urging them to return home, Mrs. Stirrey, who was much calmer than the others, though not less grieved about the child, had been questioning Elephant-Slayer and the other hunters of the country on the expediency of making an immediate search under such unfavourable circumstances. She hastened to interfere with the authority that deep conviction and sincere affection inspire.

"Brother and sister," she said firmly, "your grief bewilders you; it is impossible to attempt to do anything this evening for the poor child. Richard, I beg you to wait till to-morrow morning, if you want your search to be of any use. At this time of night, in such perfect darkness, what can be the use of going into that thick wood, full of fallen trees, and swamps, and wild beasts? Besides, the storm is only just beginning, and will certainly get worse and worse, till it will be impossible to brave it. And then, too, if you want to make sure of success, you must go wisely and thoughtfully to work. Wait till to-morrow."

"But to-morrow will be too late!" cried Elizabeth in her turn.

"They tell me that they are sure we may trust the orang's wonderful instinct to preserve our Edward from all harm, and that there will be more chance of finding him to-morrow, if we do not give the alarm to his captor this evening. Come, Richard and Elizabeth, I beg you, in the name of all that is most sacred, for the sake of the poor child himself, go home again."

"Well," said Palmer, "take Elizabeth and this child home with you; they can be of no use; but as for me, I have made up my mind. I shall go and look for my boy!"

"Richard, I will go too!" cried Elizabeth, leaning against a tree to keep herself from falling.

"And I, too!" repeated Anna.

"Nobody shall enter the forest at this time of night," said a man's voice, suddenly from among the spectators; it would be extremely imprudent and foolish, and I will not allow it!"

It was Major Grudmann, who had just arrived with Dr. Van Stetten; both having heard of the misfortune that had befallen the Palmers, the storm did not prevent them from coming to express their sympathy and offer their help.

Palmer, in spite of the gravity of his situation, reddened with anger at receiving such a positive order.

"In virtue of what right, Major Grudmann," he asked, "do you presume to impose your commands on me?"

"In virtue of the right of humanity, Mr. Palmer—the right that any man has, whoever he may be, of hindering an absurd and useless sacrifice; or, if you must have it, the right that my title of Governor and first magistrate of the colony gives. To-morrow, if you insist, you shall be at liberty to venture into those solitudes, where perhaps no human creature has penetrated before; but this evening the danger is too evident, too certain, for me to allow you to risk your life for nothing, and I hope you will consent to listen to reason."

The Governor, who thought a great deal about his authority, was a man who would have it respected at any cost. However, Richard not seeming willing to give way, Van Stetten hastened to interfere.

"Come, Palmer," he said, "yield to evidence. Other duties, other feelings, have a claim on you. Look at your wife."

In truth, now that the first excitement was over, Elizabeth's strength began to fail her rapidly; and at last she sank into the arms of her sister-in-law and Maria, murmuring:

"There's no hope! there's no hope! My child is lost!"

Richard ran to her, but she had fainted; and perhaps it was hardly to be regretted that she had lost all knowledge of what was happening.

At this moment the wind, which had only blown in gusts till now, burst forth suddenly with a violence and persistence quite alarming. Now it was plain that the intervals of calm were at an end, and that the typhoon of the Indian seas was about to display its wild and terrible power. The torches of the negroes, in spite of the tenacity of the flame, were suddenly blown out. The tops of the highest palm-trees were bent to the ground, and a great number were snapped by the tempest. In the forest there was not a green thing, from the gigantic bombax to the weakest reed, that did not seem to be uttering a moan—a cry of distress.

At the same time one would have thought that the whole sky was coming down upon the earth; the rain fell in torrents, and the clouds of leaves and dust which darkened the air were laid in a moment. Above this tremendous, universal tumult, the thunder raised its mighty voice; not that grave, majestic thunder, which roars at intervals in our temperate climates, but tropical thunder, continuous, deafening; which bursts like the explosion of a thousand cannon at once, flashing flame like a volcano, and frequently accompanied, in Sumatra, with earthquakes.

In face of these terrible convulsions of nature, man feels so small, so insignificant, that his fiercest passions are silenced at once. Such a change took place in Richard; the planter saw at last the danger of persisting, the absurdity of his hopes.

"God forbids it!" he said sorrowfully. "Poor child, forgive me for waiting a few hours before I come to your help, and for thinking of your mother first."

He raised Elizabeth, who was still fainting, in his arms.

"Sister, and you, Anna," he said firmly, "we must go home quickly. Doctor, don't leave us, I pray you, for we shall need you."

"I fear so," replied Van Stetten, sighing; "your good, kind wife had no need of this fresh shock. But go on, I will follow you."

"That's right," said Major Grudmann; "my good neighbour has turned sensible at last. Well, I must crave your hospitality tonight, for your house is the nearest, and the storm seems as if it would be no joke."

They set off at once. Nature seemed mad or intoxicated around them: every moment, great branches, or even whole trees, threatened to crush them in their fall; while at every step they were almost blown down, and several of them were carried off their feet. The rain blinded them; happily, notwithstanding the want of torches, there was no risk of losing their way in the darkness; dazzling flashes of lightning, which succeeded one another without intermission, made it as light as day, and the lightning striking several points at once, kindled fires which the wind and rain soon extinguished. The colonists walked as much as possible close to one another, that they might be better able to resist the storm. The negress Maria helped her master to carry Elizabeth, whom even these torrents of water did not revive. Mrs. Surrey had taken her daughter Anna in her arms, still crying about Edward. The others followed, helping one another as best they could, and calling out now and then in a loud, sharp tone of voice, which was the only way of making themselves heard above the tumultuous noise of the elements.

Thus they reached the end of the forest. In the open country there was less danger of being crushed by the fall of trees; but they were still more exposed to the violence of the wind there, which formed waterspouts that moved along with terrible impetuosity. The sugar and pepper plants were lying flat on the ground, as if they had been cut down; the rice-fields were completely devastated; the clove, the nutmeg, and the camphor trees were torn up by the roots: it was a dreadful disaster for the colony.

But Palmer did not trouble himself about it just then; he was only thinking of the alarming state of his wife, whose fair hair, streaming with rain, blew about in the wind. When the bluish light of the flashes lit up Elizabeth's pale face, she looked like a corpse. Every now and then, too, Palmer turned his head towards the forest. Once he even stopped suddenly: in the midst of the roaring of the tempest he thought he could distinguish the clear voice of a child—a voice that made his very heart-strings quiver. But he soon discovered his mistake, and went on.

At last they reached the house: that, too, had suffered. Several of the negroes' huts were thrown down; the wind was threatening to blow off the roofs of the other buildings; and the waters of the neighbouring cascade were beginning to overflow the garden. But Richard did not notice these ravages, any more than those in the plantations. He entered the lower room, whither most of the others followed him; an old negress, who took care of the house, bringing a light. Without laying down his precious burden, he said to the Governor in a tone of cordiality:

"I ought to apologize to you, Major Grudmann. Show that you are not offended with me, by giving your orders here as if you were at home. Dr. Van Stetten, you must come to my poor wife directly she is in bed: meanwhile, all I have is at your service. Sister, take care of yourself and your little girl. But above all," he added, raising his voice and employing the language common to the different inhabitants of New Drontheim, "don't let my servants forget that I must be in the forest before daybreak tomorrow." At the same time he carried Elizabeth to her room, leaving his guests and the other inhabitants of the house to recover as best they could from the fatigues of the evening.

CHAPTER XIII

As may easily be imagined, nobody in Palmer's house slept very quietly that night. Besides the other causes of anxiety, Elizabeth was in considerable danger, and the doctor could not leave her for a minute. Richard, too, was up all night as well as Mrs. Surrey. The sick lady had recovered from her fainting fit, but she was in a burning fever and very delirious, and Van Stetten's grave face showed the fears the kind-hearted man entertained.

The storm lasted a great part of the night; it was not till near morning that, the rain, thunder and wind having subsided, Major Grudmann and his people could leave the house to go to their own dwellings.

However, the Governor, before leaving, very thoughtfully organized a little party that, under Palmer's direction, was to begin an active search as soon as it got light. It consisted, in the first place, of Elephant-Slayer, who had an ardent desire to avenge his private wrongs on the orang, Edward's captor, and of Boa, another Malay attached to the military force of New Drontheim, who was to act as guide or scout. Boa, who was so called on account of his skill in climbing trees and in creeping through the densest thickets, had penetrated, it was said, further than any other hunter in the colony into the vast forests of the neighbourhood, and his peculiar experience could not fail to be of great use. The negro Darius, a tolerable marksman, and, above all, strongly attached to Palmer, was also to accompany his master and carry his baggage. These were all; for a greater number of persons would have been worse than useless, considering the difficulties and dangers of such an expedition.

The Governor himself took the greatest pains to point out all the steps that should be taken to provide against all contingencies, recommending that the travellers should be well armed, and supplied with provisions for several days, in case they lost their way in those unknown solitudes. Grudmann spoke himself to Elephant-Slayer and Boa, who was also in the house, particularly to the latter, and threatened them with the most terrible punishment if they gave Mr. Palmer any cause to complain of them; while he also made them the most brilliant promises in case they succeeded in bringing back father and son safe and sound to the colony. It was not till he had made all these arrangements, of which Richard was not in a state to think just then, that he consented to go home.

As soon as the first rays of light began to tinge the sky, the two Malays and Darius were up and equipped for departure. Richard, who was seated in extreme dejection at the side of his wife's bed, his face hidden in his hands, was told that they were ready. He got up in silence and went out. Five minutes after he returned in the dress that he usually wore in hunting—a hat of palm-leaves and trousers and jacket of leather, fastened tightly round the body, to prevent the thorns penetrating; he was armed with a long heavy gun, a pair of pistols, and a cutlass, intended more especially for cutting away creepers and other climbing plants. In spite of this warlike equipment, Palmer looked so pale, so sad, so crushed, that his very look inspired pity.

By the light of a candle in the room he went up to the sickbed. Since Elizabeth had recovered from her fainting fit, she had been constantly delirious, and had not spoken connectedly at all; but now, as her husband bent over her to kiss her, she opened her eyes, and said in an indescribably touching tone:

"My Richard, I shall wait for you—for him and you."

Weeping, the planter stammered out a few words, but Elizabeth did not understand him. The excitement of parting had only for a moment got the better of the illness that was preying upon her, and she became again delirious.

Palmer perceived it, and, after having given a last kiss to his poor wife, he made an effort to tear himself away from the sad spectacle. But then he felt himself gently detained by his sister and niece. Mrs. Surrey, always sensible, and understanding that any injunctions would be useless, wept in silence.

Little Anna, pale and trembling in her nightdress, said, clasping her hands:

"Oh, uncle! you will bring back Cousin Edward, won't you?"

Palmer turned away his face.

"Ask God, Anna," he said, in a hollow voice; "God alone can enable me to bring the poor child back!"

"Mind you come back, Richard," murmured Mrs. Surrey, sobbing.

"And come back quickly," added the doctor in his turn.

Richard freed himself from the embraces of his niece and sister.

"What do you mean, Van Stetten?" he asked, half distracted; "is Elizabeth in danger?"

"I hope not; but the shock has been severe, and delirium is not a good sign in this horrible climate. We shall want good news to act beneficially on her mind."

In spite of the doctor's reserve, Richard felt that his wife's very life depended on the result of his perilous enterprise; however, he was silent, gave a last kiss to his family, and went quickly out of the room.

Van Stetten followed him into the hall, where the two Malays and Darius were waiting for him; he appeared to have something to say to the planter, though he seemed rather shy of mentioning it. Richard begged him to leave his wife as little as possible during his absence.

"Trust to me," answered the doctor; "I will take up my abode here till your return. But, on your part, could you not make some observations on this animal which is so rare and so little known, the orang-outang? You can't imagine how valuable these scientific observations would be; and if you only had an opportunity of measuring its facial angle, or if you could make sure that the great toes of its feet are not opposable as some travellers maintain—"

Palmer made a gesture of impatience; but he gave the doctor's hand a last squeeze, and left the house with the three men that were to accompany him.

The country was still enveloped in darkness, but a faint light began to be visible in the sky towards the east. They hastened to reach the forest before the rising of the sun should drive the orang deeper into its recesses. The thunder and rain had ceased, although the wind was still very high, and large clouds were moving rapidly along overhead. The hunters had to walk with the greatest caution over the ground, which was strewn with rubbish: in one place there were piles of rocks or trunks of trees brought down by the torrents; a little further on there were pools of muddy water, that compelled them to leave the direct road. The whole aspect of the land had been changed in a single night; entire plantations had disappeared, deep hollows had been made in cultivated fields; anyone most familiar with these spots could never have recognised them under the layer of mud and dust, leaves, branches, and rubbish of every kind with which they were now covered.

But Richard had other things to notice. His look was frequently directed to the forest itself, over which the first rays of light were just appearing, and sometimes his eye rested on the bold men whom he had chosen to share his toils and dangers, as if he was considering what degree of confidence he might place in them.

The negro and the two Malays were dressed in almost the same manner as Palmer was, with coats of thick leather, fastened tightly round the body; contrary to their usual custom, they wore boots, or rather sandals, to protect their feet from the thorns or the sharp points of the rocks. Besides their long guns, pistols, and *krises*, or curved cutlasses, they were loaded with provisions and such baggage as could not be dispensed with on such an excursion. Boa might have been about forty, an advanced age in that fatal climate, and his height was rather below the average. However, his iron muscles, which stood out beneath his olive-brown skin, showed that he was possessed of considerable vigour. The most perfect harmony seemed to exist between him and Elephant-Slayer, not that such men were likely to experience those feelings of humanity and pity that might have sustained them in their enterprise, but they counted on sharing the reward promised if they succeeded in their attempt, safe to fight when the time for dividing it came. Only the negro, Darius, faced the danger out of devotion to his master and the lost child. Unfortunately, Darius was the weakest, and the least experienced of the three, and perhaps he might himself require help from his bolder companions.

On the recommendation of the Governor, Boa had brought with him an ally, whose services under the circumstances were not to be despised. This was a large dog, with a shaggy coat, with a ferocious but at the same time intelligent face. This dog wore round his neck a collar ornamented with points, and he was held in with a thick leathern thong. Endowed with an excellent scent, he went along with his nose close to the ground, and when he discovered the track of the fallow deer that the storm had driven from their retreat during the night, he pulled at his leash and growled, and his master had some difficulty in making him leave the track. Such as it was, the little band seemed exactly suited to the exigencies of the situation, and, under the direction of Palmer, could scarcely fail of success in their object, if, however, this object were not beyond the reach of human effort.

In spite of all these turnings and of the difficulties in their way, they reached the forest before the first glimpse of the sun became visible on the horizon. The waterspouts had thrown down numbers of trees; the giant ferns and brushwood were beaten down in some places, as if they had been trampled under foot by herds of elephants; the ground was strewn with broken branches, and all the hollow places were filled with muddy water, full of sand and *débris*. The bombax itself, that giant which had borne all the changes of the seasons during so many centuries, had not escaped; the lightning had broken the top of it, split its sturdy trunk, and scattered its magnificent bunches of purple flowers to the winds.

It was, however, towards this tree, in which the orang had been last seen the evening before, that the hunters directed their way. As he approached it, Richard perceived that he was walking over the ruins of the *krouboul*, the wonderful flower that had attracted his son two days before to the fatal spot, and he uttered a melancholy sigh at the remembrance.

The Malays consulted together about the direction they should take; but it was not thought prudent to proceed further into the wood while it was still so dark. Happily, it was not necessary to wait long; the light soon broke forth and rendered the outline of surrounding objects clearly visible. The sun was hidden from view by the masses of dark clouds which still covered the sky; but it was now possible to see the difficulties and dangers of the road, and the singing of a few birds, heard above the moans of the rustling of the dying wind, told that nature was waking up again after the frightful convulsions of the night. Then Boa turned to Darius, and said to him, abruptly:

"The child's frock!" The negro took something of small size from his bag; and Richard recognised, with a mixture of emotion and surprise, one of his child's garments.

"What are you going to do with that?" he asked in a stifled voice.

"Massa go see," answered Darius.

And he gave the garment to Boa. The latter took it and made his dog smell it.

"I understand," cried Palmer; "that is a good idea! Oh, if the fine fellow could only find any trace of Edward!"

The two Malays beckoned to him to remain perfectly silent, and Boa said to the dog, "Now look."

The animal sniffed the different smells with which the air was loaded, and seemed to hesitate for some minutes; but he soon turned towards the forest, sniffed again in a very noisy fashion, and concluded by looking fixedly in the same direction, tugging at the leash and wagging his tail and ears.

"He has found the scent," pronounced Boa.

No words could express Palmer's pleasure; his heart beat violently, and he was on the point of speaking when Elephant-Slayer stopped him again.

"Don't speak," he said, in a low tone, "or the orang will run away with Edward directly. We must walk quietly; the man of the woods will hear the least sound, and perhaps he will try to defend the child; a single blow from his club might stretch one of us dead who least expected it."

Richard, seeing the wisdom of these precautions, did not reply; he examined the lock of his gun, and, having told Darius to keep close to him, he went after Elephant-Slayer and Boa, who had already followed the dog into the wood.

Instead of keeping his nose close to the ground, as hounds generally do, he held his head up and sniffed from time to time. Several times he was just going to bark, but a push at his collar from Boa always put a stop to such dangerous intentions.

He entered the forest at a point where the trees were very thick, and where to all appearance it was perfectly impossible for a human being to follow. But Boa, as if he wished to justify his surname, glided behind the dog and disappeared in silence among the thorny shrubs. The other hunters discovered a less difficult passage, though even there they could only crawl in one by one. At some distance from the edge of the forest the trees did not grow so close to one another, and were less vigorous from the want of air and sun. Still they made little way, and so great were the difficulties, that at the end of half-an-hour they were not more than five or six hundred paces from the great bombax.

They soon found themselves in a glade filled with rugged blocks of basalt piled up without any order. Tree-ferns and gigantic grass, which seemed to belong to the vegetation of the antediluvian period, partially concealed these picturesque rocks, in the clefts of which some of the lovely flowers were growing that we cultivate at great expense in our hot-houses. Around this spot immense creepers were hanging in festoons from the palm-trees, ebony-trees, pines, and casuarinas, and formed innumerable arches of verdure; a few of the trees had been blown down, some by the recent storm, others by the storms of former days, or they had fallen from age; but they were all buried beneath a mass of climbing plants and those splendid parasitic orchids that grow on old trunks. A few birds of all the colours of precious stones, parroquets, humming-birds, woodpeckers, flew about round these sweet flowers, still wet with rain, and a sweet smell filled the air, such as is often noticed in gardens after a storm.

At this spot the dog quickened his pace, wagged his tail violently, and would have barked if his master had not stopped him by pulling his leash roughly. But while he watched the hound, Boa gave his companions a sign to be on their guard, and got his own gun ready.

Everything proved that the child and his captor were not far off, and it became more and more necessary to be prudent. The orang had perhaps perceived the hunters; possibly he was already hiding in some lurking-place with his terrible club. They were obliged to keep a constant look-out on the right hand and on the left, and they examined the foliage above them incessantly, for death might fall upon them like a thunder-bolt.

The hunters, wading through the high grass, and surmounting a thousand obstacles, listened to the slightest movement, to the least noise. A leaf blown about by the wind, a woodpecker knocking its beak against a bit of rotten wood, a little monkey playing among the creepers, made them turn their heads quickly and stop, till they had discovered the cause of their alarm. They were absorbed in this important examination, when Boa, who was a few steps in advance, stopped all at once, and, resting the butt-end of his gun on the ground, made a sign to them to approach. They hastened to him, and, reassured by his calm attitude, they relaxed their vigilance a little. At the foot of an enormous rock which jutted out, was a rather deep recess, where several persons might have found shelter during the storm of the preceding night. Now it was plain that this kind of niche had been occupied recently; a great quantity of dry moss formed the bed, large pine-leaves had been brought there to serve for a covering. The remains of some cocoa-nuts and several other wild fruits were scattered about, as if to prove that those who had sought a temporary retreat under this rock had not left without having breakfasted.

CHAPTER XIV

Here it was that Boa was examining something with great care, and he held back the hound with a strong hand; for he was stretching out his neck, and trying to trample on this rustic couch. When the other hunters came up to him, the Malay, moving the leaves carefully, pointed out the distinct impression made by two figures on the moss. He put his finger on each of them, one after the other, and said, in a tone of triumph:

"Here the orang—there, Edward."

Elephant-Slayer and Darius seemed convinced of the truth of this remark, but Palmer seemed to doubt it.

"Impossible!" he said: "here we are not more than half a mile from the great bombax, at the foot of which we halted yesterday evening. If my child and this horrible ape had spent the night in this place, they must have heard our shouts, and Edward would certainly have answered."

"And the wind and the rain!" said the Malay. "But master will see."

At the same minute he loosened his hold on the dog, which began eagerly to smell the bed of moss. Very soon the sagacious animal, as if he wished to confirm Boa's assertions, drew from uuder the leaves a little piece of stuff which Richard, with tears, recognised as having formed part of his child's dress.

"It is true, then, that the orang has spared his life!" he cried.

"But look closely, my good fellows: do you see anything to show that Edward is ill, or wounded?"

The Malays again examined the moss bit by bit; they could see no trace of blood, and among the remains of fruit scattered round the rock they found several that, without any doubt, had been nibbled by a smaller and more delicate mouth than that of the wild man of the woods. They concluded from these different circumstances that not only Edward had no serious wound, but also that, in spite of the terror he must have felt, he had not lost his appetite.

"But, then, where is he?" asked Palmer anxiously.

"Not far off," replied Boa; "the bed is still warm. No noise." Already the dog had left the hollow of the rock, and was prowling about with his nose on the ground, as if he had found a regular track. There was reason then to believe that the child, on leaving the spot where he had spent the night side by side with his savage guardian, had been allowed to walk, and that if they followed the track patiently they might succeed in finding him. However, this hope was not of long continuance. The track came to an end when they reached a mass of fallen and decayed trees, such as so young a child could not have climbed over without help, and there it ended abruptly.

At this point, doubtless, the orang had taken Edward in his arms and carried him from tree to tree through the air, the path on the ground presenting too many difficulties for him.

The certainty of this dismayed the hunters; but the Malays, after having examined the place attentively, guessed, with some sagacity, the direction the thief must have chosen. They went round several obstacles in their way, and when they reached a piece of ground where it was more easy to walk, the dog all at once found the track he had lost.

Boa wanted to prove in different ways the reality of this important result; but the hound seemed sure of the fact and hastened his steps, with his nose on the ground as before. In a short time there was no longer any room for doubt: in a spot where the streams of water had left the sand damp, two parallel lines of footmarks were plainly visible; one was that of an enormous foot with the great toe very wide asunder from the rest of the foot, and of a peculiar formation, the other was evidently that of a child. Both looked so fresh that they could only have been made a few minutes ago. Richard could not control his joy.

"My God!" he murmured, raising his tearful eyes to heaven, "wilt Thou indeed in Thy wisdom restore him to us?"

But his companions again begged him to be silent; and it was plain from their anxious looks that, in spite of these more favourable appearances, they did not consider success certain by any means. They set forward again, following now a kind of path that seemed to have been traced by some large animal, an ordinary inhabitant of these solitudes. This path was uncertain and irregular, interrupted frequently by stumps of trees and creeping plants. They could not see more than a few steps before them, and were completely ignorant how far distant they were from the orang and his prisoner. However, the dog showed more and more eagerness, and from moment to moment they hoped to come in sight of them. So the hunters followed Boa very cautiously, looking carefully around and with their fingers on the triggers of their guns.

This perseverance was not to be unrewarded. At the end of the path these courageous adventurers entered a part of the forest that was very grand and majestic, and there they found the reward of their labours.

Trees, of prodigious size, growing at regular intervals, supported a triple vaulting of foliage, through which the still feeble, slanting light could hardly penetrate. They might have been taken for the grand pillars that adorn Gothic cathedrals; thousands of years must probably have been required for the wonderful development of these gnarled trunks and roots. There were echoes under this vaulted roof as there are in great buildings, and the chattering, of the parrots that were playing about on the border of this gloomy part, without daring to enter it, was repeated in a very mournful fashion. Through the thick mass of branches and leaves it was impossible to see the least bit of sky; So all the flowering, sweet-smelling plants that require air and light had disappeared, even the parasite strangle weeds and the brilliant-coloured orchis that grows everywhere in the Sumatran forests. Nothing grew on the ground but yellowish lichens, mixed with fungi, and other cryptogamic plants of odd shapes, lovers of damp and darkness.

Now, in the pale light that just penetrated the depths of the forest, the hunters at length discovered two shadows, moving about a hundred paces before them; their practised eyes were not slow in recognising the orang and Edward. The man of the woods, made conspicuous by his great height and long arms, was advancing slowly, leaning on a stick, that served him at once for support and defence. At his side Edward, without a hat and with his clothes torn, was walking listlessly, sobbing incessantly, as naughty children do who are tired of crying; these sobs, repeated by the echo, made a constant, melancholy murmur that it was heartbreaking to hear. However, the man of the woods did not appear to be ill-treating his little companion in any way; on the contrary, he seemed to be very careful of him. He stopped every now and then to wait for him; the child's hands were still full of wild fruit and edible berries, that his captor had gathered for him from the trees they passed. The orang seemed to take pains to spare him all fatigue, and to save him from all danger; he often stroked his back in a caressing way. The affection he so evidently felt for him rendered the hunters enterprise the more perilous; for it was plain the orang would not give up the prey that was so dear to him without a fight.

At the sight of his son Palmer uttered a faint cry; but a quick sign from Darius, and an imperious look from the two Malays, reminded him that he must restrain his feelings. Happily, the rustling of the wind, as it blew through the long avenues of trees, smothered this exclamation, which was drawn from him by a feeling that he could not resist; certainly the orang, whose sense of hearing is extremely fine, had not heard it, for he did not turn round. However, he might look behind him at any moment, simply from his natural distrust; and, as the hunters had no means of hiding themselves, everything would be lost if he did.

It was necessary to decide what to do at once; the orang and the child were going further away; and it seemed equally impossible to pursue them openly or to surprise them on this piece of bare ground. Palmer and his men threw themselves flat on the ground, behind a forsaken ant-hill, and Boa hastened to muzzle his dog, whose services were not required just then; and, while one of them kept an eye on every movement of the orang, the others set themselves to deliberate.

A plan was soon agreed upon. They decided that Palmer and the negro should continue the pursuit straight on, gliding from tree to tree, and using every precaution not to be noticed by the suspicious animal; meanwhile Boa and Elephant-Slayer were to try, by going a little way round, to reach, before the orang did, a clump of cocoanut-trees, situated at some distance, towards which he and his little captive were directing their steps; thus the orang would find himself hemmed in, and they might be able to rescue Edward. This plan presented many difficulties, but it was the only practicable one, and they set to work at once to put it into execution.

The Malays retraced their steps for a little way, and, then plunging into the bushy thicket, were not long in disappearing. On their part, Richard and Darius lost no time; they went forward, stooping and taking advantage of every obstacle in the way to hide themselves. The mosses and lichens, with which the ground was covered, favoured this manouvre, for they deadened the sound of their footsteps. On getting near enough to shoot, they were to fire at the orang without waiting for their companions; but it would not do for them to be in too great a hurry, or to fire from too great a distance; for, in that case, they ran the risk of hitting the child, or of only slightly wounding the orang, which would certainly make him more formidable still.

In spite of their efforts they gained very little ground on the two they were pursuing. Every minute they were obliged to stop to keep out of sight of the man of the woods, who seemed uneasy, as if his instinct had warned him of the existence of danger. This going backwards and forwards retarded their progress considerably, and made the poor father most terribly impatient.

However, the orang and Edward had reached the end of that part of the forest that might be called the dark part, and they were just coming to the clump of cocoanut-trees.

A dazzling light now shone upon them, and they could be distinctly seen in spite of the distance. All at once they stopped; Palmer was afraid at first that they had taken alarm, but the calm attitude of the orang reassured him. However, this halt was soon explained; the orang lay down on the ground at the edge of a little pool of water, and began to drink as if he was very thirsty; while Edward, more particular, filled his hand with water and carried it several times to his lips to quench his raging thirst.

The moment was a precious one; Richard and the negro, casting aside every precaution, dashed forward. They rushed over the space between them; but Palmer ran much faster than Darius, who, being loaded with heavy baggage, was soon left behind.

Palmer thought no more of waiting, and ran till he was almost out of breath; but he was obliged to stop again. The orang got up and looked around with a frightened look. The planter lay down till his enemy should go on his way again; he was trembling with anger, and squeezed his gun convulsively in his hands; but he was too far off to venture to fire. Then followed a few minutes of intense anxiety. Would the orang continue to walk with the child, or would he carry his prey into the trees and proceed in what seemed to be his favourite mode of travelling? Chance, or rather Providence, ordered things better than Palmer could have hoped.

The cocoanuts, at the foot of which was the pool of water, were loaded with beautiful-looking ripe fruit. The orang, with that suddenness of determination that distinguishes the quadruman, threw down his club and began to climb one of the trees with the evident intention of gathering some of the nuts. The child remained alone at the edge of the water, but, not knowing where to go, he was obliged to wait for his conductor, and sat down on the ground, still crying quietly.

Palmer then continued his course with frantic impetuosity. He was almost choked with his emotion; his temples throbbed and his heart beat violently against his chest. His son, his lost child, the hope and joy of his home, was there before him; he was going to touch him, to press him in his arms, and after this nothing but death should ever part them. Darius, who had rejoined his master, showed no less ardour. To be able to run more quickly, he had thrown down his heavy burden on the moss, and, armed with nothing but his gun, he stood ready to lay down his life in the moment of danger.

Richard was already within a short distance of his son, and was able to notice certain heart-rending particulars that had escaped him till then. The poor little fellow's clothes were in tatters;

his eyes red and sunken, and his pale, wearied face as well as his hands were furrowed with scratches, from which the orang, in spite of all his care, had not been able to preserve him. In his attitude there was a dejection, a sadness, a despair, that no words could express; yet, with the curiosity of his age, he watched the movements of his captor in the neighbouring tree, or looked absently at the cocoanuts falling with great noise into the pool of water.

Richard was convinced that his son's rescue was certain. Before the orang had come down from the tree, Edward would be safe under his father's protection. The planter, breathless and almost wild with joy, stretched out his hands to him, and, as the child was still looking at the top of the tree, he cried to him in an almost inaudible voice:

"Edward! my dear little Edward!I"

"Massa Edward!" cried Darius, in his turn.

This time the child heard; he turned his head quickly.

Recognising his father and Darius, a smile of indescribable joy overspread his face. He rose quickly and began to run to them, crying:

"Oh, papa, dear papa, I knew you would come and help me!" But these imprudent exclamations and unguarded movements ruined everything. As the father and son were on the point of rushing into one another's arms, a kind of hairy phantom threw itself between them, uttering a hoarse guttural cry.

Palmer and Darius, who had followed him closely, were thrown down in spite of their strength and before they had time to think.

At the same time the orang, for it was he that had dropped thus suddenly from the top of the cocoanut-tree, seized the poor child, who struggled and cried piteously; then, taking hold of the trunk of a neighbouring tree, he climbed to the top with incredible rapidity and disappeared once more.

For a moment yet a voice, growing weaker and weaker and more distant, cried out among the leaves:

"Papa! help! Oh, papa, papa!"

CHAPTER XV

But Richard could not hear him; his head had been thrown with so much force against a stump that he lay without moving on the grass, bleeding both from mouth and nose. Darius, less hurt, was only stunned for a minute. Coming to himself, he raised his gun to his shoulder and fired at random. But the orang was already far away, and the child's cries could be heard no more in the gloomy silence of the woods.

At the sound of the firing, the two Malays issued from the brushwood, and ran to the scene of this sudden and dreadful disaster. They had been delayed, on their part, by the ordinary difficulties of such a forest. However, they had seen the orang on the cocoanut-tree very well, and they were advancing, creeping through the long grass, and intending to send a couple of balls into his body at the moment the catastrophe took place. They showed no sympathy for Palmer, still lying insensible, and when the negro told them what had happened they were very angry with Darius as well as his master. According to them, before running to the child, he should have fired at the orang; they were going to kill him themselves, or at least wound him severely, when the foolish haste of the other two had disconcerted their maneuvers. In vain Darius pleaded the fatherly love that had made Palmer forget all ideas of prudence; how could he make such a feeling intelligible to these fierce natives—loving nothing, respecting nothing, fearing nothing? Instead of listening to his explanations, they abused the poor negro with violent words and gestures. However, the orang could not be very far off yet, and in the hope of finding him again, they set out in pursuit with the dog, leaving the faithful servant free to attend to his fainting master.

Darius fetched a little water from the pool near, and poured it on Richard's face, but it was some time before Palmer came to himself; and, when he did open his eyes, he looked round wildly, and hardly seemed to know where he was.

"Ah, massa!" said Darius; "it have been very lucky that the man who does not speak had not got his club, or we be killed on the spot. Now you drink this." And he held out to him a gourd full of rum. Richard swallowed a few drops, and then his memory seemed to return.

"And Edward? Where is Edward?" he asked abruptly.

Darius reminded him of the sad truth.

On learning that Elephant-Slayer and Boa had already started in search of the orang, Richard exclaimed:

"I must go after them at once! I will not leave to others the task of saving my son! poor little fellow, he was looking out for me, counting on my coming, and calling to me to help him!"

He tried to rise; but no doubt the shock he had received had injured some vital part, for he fell back directly.

"Master, you not well yet," said the negro affectionately, "you wait here and rest. The Malays come back soon, and then all together we go and look for Massa Edward."

Palmer was obliged to yield to his fate; but, overcome with the feeling of his powerlessness, he hid his face in his hands and shed many tears.

At the end of about half-an-hour Elephant-Slayer and Boa returned, gloomy and discontented; they had found no trace of the orang, and they had not heard Edward's voice. Palmer asked them what could be done.

They answered sulkily that the enterprise had failed, and that, according to all appearances, the opportunity that had been lost would not occur again. Now that the wild man of the woods had been put on his guard, he would run away with his victim, without stopping a minute, and would not put a foot to the ground till he was a very long way off.

"And you cannot think," said Boa, "how large the forest is. It would take twenty days, thirty days, or perhaps more, to get to the end of it. How then can we find the orang?" And he and his companion concluded that they must leave Edward to his fate, and go back to the colony. The feeling of indignation gave Palmer new strength.

"What!" he said, leaning on his elbow, "shall I give up the hope of saving my child the very first day, the very first hour? Shall I give way thus to the first obstacle? I thought Elephant-Slayer and Boa were bolder, more used to fatigue; but they are tired and disheartened already; let them go; I must stay alone; I shall not go back."

"Master," said Darius, "me follow you to death." The planter's reproaches offended the Malays. Palmer would have done better to have reminded them of the reward that was promised them in case of success, and he continued:

"The orang will come down to the ground again soon. He seemed to be very fond of my child, and when he sees him out of breath and hurt with these incessant bounds, he will have pity on him, and will leave the top of the trees, I am sure. You know as well, or better than I do, the instinct of these orangs, an instinct that is almost equal to reason!"

"The orangs are men who will not speak," replied Boa, repeating the generally admitted opinion of the Malays; "they have much more reason than some men who do speak."

"God grant they have also a feeling of compassion for weakness," said Richard, sighing. "Now, will you follow me?"

He added everything he could think of to persuade them to continue the search, and though neither of them expected any good results from a fresh attempt, they announced that they were ready to start.

By a strong effort of will, Richard managed to get on his feet without Darius's help. He tottered, and had frightful pain in his head, but he concealed his sufferings, for fear of discouraging his companions still more.

They returned to the pool of water on the border of which the catastrophe had taken place. The Malays examined the spot carefully, made the dog scent the quite recent trace of the child and his captor, and, after they had settled their plans, set out again.

On they went for a long time; on—on till evening, getting deeper and deeper into the solitary forest. As they proceeded the forest grew more and more wild, and they entered parts that had certainly never been trodden by any human creature before. Sometimes they met wild beasts, which fortunately did not dream of attacking the little band; and they, on their part, took care not to irritate them. They only spoke in monosyllables and in a low voice; they took care not to make any noise, and stopped occasionally to listen in these silent and majestic solitudes. But they heard nothing more either of the orang or Edward; and they could not discover any trace of them. The dog himself, though they frequently gave him the lost child's dress to smell, did not seem any longer to understand what they wanted him to do; and after hunting about for a minute or two to quiet his conscience, went after the track of some deer or other. It seemed certain that if the orang had come down from the tree after the last alarm, he had not done so till he was a long way off, and in some inaccessible place near which the hunters had not chanced to come.

About an hour before sunset, they were all completely exhausted. They had made this journey for the most part on their hands and knees, or else they had had to cut a passage for themselves through the creepers with their cutlasses. Long thorns had pierced through their leathern clothes, some of which were considered poisonous; their hands and faces were torn; thousands of insects, eager for blood, mosquitoes, gnats, and immense wasps, persisted in following them, forming a kind of buzzing cloud around them. Besides, during the day they had not been able to stop for any meal, and had contented themselves with eating some fruit gathered from the trees of the forest; they were now extremely hungry, and their hunger was partly the cause of their extreme prostration.

But none of them were in such a deplorable condition as Palmer, the leader of the expedition. His excessive fatigue and his agony of mind had aggravated his sufferings, till they were almost unbearable. A burning fever consumed him: at times a thick mist came over his eyes, and he could hardly see his way; at others his mind was confused, and he neither knew what he wanted nor where he was going. So that, towards the end of the day, in spite of his courage, he was obliged to lean on Darius to get on at all, and without the help of that devoted negro he would have been left behind long before.

The necessity of finding some shelter for the night was now urgent. The Malays themselves could not tell where they were; all day the sky had been covered with clouds, and then the trees were so thick that they found it impossible to guide themselves by the position of the sun. They only knew that they were far, very far, from any human habitation, and they had no choice but to encamp in the middle of the wood. Now, a storm no less terrible than that of the evening before was brewing, and it was time to stop and construct some kind of shelter.

This was not an easy thing to do. They must find an open spot, clear the ground in order to destroy the dangerous insects, build a hut with the branches and leaves, and gather sufficient wood to keep up a fire large enough to frighten away the wild beasts during the night, and these labours seemed very formidable to men half dead with fatigue.

However, when they told Palmer that they must stop he would not hear of it; according to him, there was no hurry; they might still go on, and perhaps at last they would overtake the objects of their pursuit. But the Malays took no notice of his entreaties, and, while the unhappy father was lying stretched on the grass under the charge of the negro, they considered how they might provide for their present urgent necessities.

The place where they had halted did not seem well suited for an encampment. It was a kind of wide path, made by the frequent passing to and fro of a herd of large animals, either buffaloes or elephants; and what should they do if these formidable herds, which go about particularly at night, should burst upon the travellers when they were fast asleep? Besides, the hunters were dying of thirst; they must discover some water. The two Malays went off therefore in different directions to seek some more convenient spot in the neighbourhood. At the end of a few minutes Elephant-Slayer returned without having succeeded, and sat down at a distance from the others to wait for his companion. The latter was not long in returning, escorted by his dog, who was now allowed to roam at liberty. Doubtless Boa had been more happy in his search, for he simply said:

"Come, all of you."

Elephant-Slayer followed him without asking any explanation; but it was not so easy for Richard to obey the summons. In this short interval of rest he had grown heavy with sleep and could not rise. However, with Darius's help he managed to get on his feet, and dragged himself along behind the rest, uttering groans that were wrung from him by the frightful pains he was enduring.

They proceeded about a hundred paces in this way. Boa had chosen a glade surrounded with gigantic trees for a place of encampment. There was a pond in the middle filled by the rain of the preceding night, yet the water was both limpid and fresh. But what struck the hunters most was the sight of three or four huts made of boughs and covered with leaves, fixed on some large projecting roots. These huts, without doors or windows, and constructed in a very rough fashion, were a great help to people who had neither time nor strength to build others. One of them was perched on a pandanus-tree in the fork of two branches, like the nest of an enormous bird. But this style of building was not at all peculiar in a country where the greater number of the dwellings are built on piles, as we have seen was the case with the Malay houses of New Drontheim. Palmer, though almost exhausted with fatigue and suffering, examined these singular constructions with curiosity.

"How could human beings," he said, with an effort, "establish themselves in these melancholy solitudes?"

"Not men from the colonies," answered Boa shortly, "but men who do not speak."

"What!" cried Palmer; "these huts have been built and occupied by orangs?"

The two Malays answered in the affirmative.

"Then let us stay here; the inhabitants of these cabins will certainly return, and perhaps the one that has stolen my son will be among them."

But Boa made them notice that the huts appeared to have been deserted for a long time. The palm-leaves with which they were roofed were crumbling to dust; the heaps of moss that served for a bed inside were swarming with centipedes, wood-lice, scorpions, and other venomous creatures. The remains of cocoa-nuts were scattered about in plenty, but they were rotten and decayed. One of the clubs that apes of a large kind carry had been left in the principal hut, and looked as if it had been there for a year. In fact, there was no reason to hope that these huts had been visited lately by the old proprietors. However, it was necessary to establish themselves there for the night; the storm was rising, the sky was growing darker and darker; there was not a minute to lose. Boa busied himself in covering two of the huts with fresh leaves, and put fresh moss instead of that full of insects. On his part Elephant-Slayer set himself to pile up a supply of dry wood and to cut down the grass round the encampment.

These different labours, thanks to the peculiar experience of the two Malays, were soon finished. In a short time Richard was settled on a soft bed in the principal hut. Darius was to remain with his master, while Boa and Elephant-Slayer occupied a hut near. The Malays and the negro had agreed to watch by turns during the night.

They made a good supper round the fire, which just then had the double advantage of giving light to the hunters and driving away the mosquitoes. As to Richard, though he had taken nothing since the evening before, he could only swallow a few drops of the milk of the cocoa-nut which the negro brought him. He had fallen into a kind of stupor, and, panting for breath, with his eyes closed, he constantly uttered involuntary groans.

Night came, and with it the expected storm. The hunters retreated hastily into the huts; torrents of water streamed from the sky, and the thunder roared incessantly. In a few minutes the bivouac fire was completely extinguished, and it was impossible to light it again during the pouring rain. This was another danger; for nothing but the fire could keep off the wild beasts; but in spite of the violent commotions of the elements, all the tired hunters slept, except the one on guard.

CHAPTER XVI

The storm lasted all night, and it was owing to this circumstance perhaps that they were not attacked by the inhabitants of this primeval forest, for wild beasts seem to lose some of their ferocity during the great convulsions of nature. They were only alarmed once, and that was while Boa was on duty. The dog, which was sleeping near his master, suddenly raised his head and uttered a low growl. Boa, knowing well what this meant, seized his gun and looked carefully around him. At less than twenty paces a fixed, steady pair of eyes were shining in the darkness. Without a moment's hesitation, he shouldered his gun and drew the trigger; a howl followed. The Malay, after having fired, drew his kris, expecting to see the furious animal spring at him; but there was no movement during the rest of the night.

The report of the gun and the howling of the monster were so blended with the roaring of the tempest that the sleep of the other hunters was not even disturbed. Only when Boa went in the morning to see what effect his shot bad produced, he found under the brushwood large stains of blood that the pouring rain had not completely effaced; no doubt some royal tiger had experienced for the first time in his solitude the dominant power of man.

At daybreak the Malays and the negro, being rested and in good health, were quite ready to resume the search. Unhappily, the leader of the expedition was no longer in a condition to direct or even to be of any use to his companions. His flushed countenance and wild eyes proved the progress of fever; they called him, but he did not seem to hear; they tried to put him on his feet, but he fell back like a senseless lump. They pressed him with questions, but he only answered with inarticulate sounds; he could no longer think, feel, or understand. What was to be done? Boa and Elephant-Slayer, as hard-hearted towards other people as they were careless of themselves, wanted to leave the sick man to his fate; they talked of returning to the colony, leaving Palmer and the negro to do what they could. But Darius employed all his eloquence to persuade them to abandon such a selfish intention; he reminded them particularly of the express injunctions of the Governor; he told them that if they abandoned "Massa Palmer" in this way the Major would have them hung or shot as soon as they appeared in New Drontheim: in fact, he employed such arguments that the Malays at last became more tractable.

It was agreed that they two alone should follow the track of the orang during the day that had just begun, while Darius remained in the hut with the sick man. Slayer and Boa were to return in the evening, after beating the surrounding parts of the wood; and, if their investigations were in vain, they would consider about returning home the next morning. No doubt Palmer, after having enjoyed absolute rest, would recover his consciousness, and would be able to say what he wished. This plan settled, one of the Malays climbed a tree to see where they were, and that they might be able to find the huts again later in the day. After making his observations, he rejoined his comrade, and they both plunged once more into the wood, followed by the hound.

Darius now remained alone with his master, and the day seemed to him interminable. It continued to rain heavily, though the storm had ceased, and the water was trickling through the roof of the hut. The sick man did not seem to mind it; on the contrary, he placed his burning forehead mechanically under the little stream of water that was dripping down drop by drop, and it appeared to relieve him. He did not speak a word to Darius, and hardly seemed to know him; but at times he got much excited, and in his delirium talked in a most heart-breaking manner. Sometimes he thought he saw his son, and lavished the most tender caresses on him; sometimes he called his dear Elizabeth; and began to comfort her in the most affectionate way. Joy, hope, and terror, seemed to bring gentle or terrible forms before his troubled mind by turns.

Then, exhausted by these violent attacks, he sank again into a state of gloomy torpor, which lasted till the next fit of delirium came on.

In the evening the two Malays returned, very tired and wet to the skin. They had not seen the orang, and had given up all hope of finding poor Edward again. They could not think of penetrating further into these endless forests. They had been attacked by one of the black bears that feed upon palm-trees, and after having fired both their guns at him and wounded him, they put an end to him with their *krises*.

Then one of them had been pursued by a buffalo, and had been obliged to double to escape the ferocious animal. And, lastly, a few leagues from the huts there was a large swamp full of crocodiles and great snakes, and this appeared to be an insuperable barrier. Slayer and Boa had walked along its edge for a long time without finding any way across, and, to all appearance, no such way existed. It was therefore desirable to begin the retreat at once; especially as the rainy season, which had just commenced, might, if they waited too long, render their return very difficult and very dangerous, if not impossible.

These reasons were decisive, and Darius had nothing to answer, except that his master was quite incapable of walking. However he wished to wait till the next day, before he came to any definite decision, hoping that Palmer's condition would improve in the night.

But the night was still more distressing than the previous one. The sick man tossed about incessantly, and at times his delirium almost amounted, to frenzy. On the other hand, the rain still continued to fall, and threatened to inundate the country. During this night again they had not been able to light any fire, and tigers prowled about continually, roaring frightfully. They were obliged to keep a good lookout and to fire their guns from time to time to drive them away, so that when the first rays of light appeared not one of the hunters had had a moment's rest.

Yet they had need to recruit their strength for the fresh exertions that were awaiting them. There was now, indeed, no doubt what must be done; it was plainly necessary to abandon the child to his fate and return to the colony without loss of time. The provisions were completely exhausted, and they had nothing to depend upon but the wild fruits of the forest.

Their clothes were in rags, their feet bleeding, their bodies wounded with thorns, and half devoured by the greedy insects of the woods. An immediate retreat was unavoidable, and as Palmer was too ill to walk, he must be carried.

It was not without difficulty that Darius persuaded the Malays to do this; he was again obliged to have recourse to threats and promises, for they positively refused to burden themselves with the sick man. At last they reluctantly consented, and immediate preparations for departure were made. They formed a kind of litter for Richard out of some branches, and then, having breakfasted on a fat lizard, which they ate raw, as they could not light a fire, they left the orangs' huts.

It may easily be imagined that the journey could not be accomplished without almost unheard-of exertions. The bearers of the litter had frequently to walk over swampy ground or through tangled brushwood, while the third hunter cut a passage for them with his knife. They were constantly obliged to leave the straight path to avoid deep pools, or else masses of prickly shrubs that could only be destroyed by fire. In this manner they doubled the distance, and, to add to their misfortunes, they frequently lost their way, in spite of the sagacity of the Malays in discovering their whereabouts in these solitudes. Several times over Boa and Elephant-Slayer sat down, refusing to proceed any further, and threatened to stab poor Darius, who exhorted them to take courage.

At times the faithful servant himself almost lost heart, and began to think, too, that the task was beyond his strength. His body was one large wound; he was dying of hunger, and could hardly put his bleeding feet to the ground. However, these fits of despondency did not last long; he soon recovered his courage, and, when he saw one of his comrades growing faint, he went and harnessed himself to the litter with renewed ardour.

But if the sufferings of the hunters were terrible, those of Richard cannot be described. Tossed about in the middle of briars and thorns, without being able to push them aside, drenched with rain, consumed by fever, he could do nothing but groan every now and then. Even these groans became weaker and weaker, and towards the end of the day they ceased altogether. At one time Darius thought it was all over with his master; but when he put his hand on Palmer's heart, he could feel slight beatings. It was plain they must hasten forward, if they did not intend this last spark of life to be extinguished.

During this direful retreat Boa's dog was a great help. Several times he found the road again when they had lost it; several times he gave the alarm when some evil beasts were about to spring on the defenceless hunters. And it was he that announced their arrival at the colony by barking joyfully.

It was time; the sun was setting amid blood-red clouds, and if the travellers had had to pass another night in the forest, without food or shelter, probably not one of them would have returned from the perilous expedition. However, their strength seemed to revive when they found themselves in beaten paths, and perceived signs around them that they were approaching the dwellings of men, such is the wonderful influence that the mind has on the body. Their bent forms grew erect, and they carried their burden more cheerfully.

But the sick man gave no sign of joy: he was completely insensible.

As the little band entered the fields, the Chinamen belonging to Palmer's house had just finished their work, and were preparing to return home. Several, with the cool indifference of their nation, noticed the piteous condition of the hunters without dreaming of asking what had happened, or offering to help them. But Elephant-Slayer did not intend to put up with this; he gave a sign to Darius, who was helping to carry Palmer just then, and they deposited the litter on the ground. Then the Malay seized hold of the two Chinamen that were nearest to him by their long tails. In spite of their protestations and resistance, he harnessed them to the litter, saying, with one hand on his *kris*:

"He is your master, too. It is your turn." And the Chinamen, one of whom was our old acquaintance Yaw, were obliged to take the place of the bearers as far as the house; while the latter, completely worn out and tottering, followed them with difficulty.

It was night when they reached the house. At the news of their return people ran out to meet them with torches. They dared not ask any questions, but they gazed at them eagerly. Their piteous appearance was significant enough; a few words from Darius made them fully acquainted with the ill-success of the enterprise. Then the negro, in his turn, asked after Mrs. Palmer.

"Ah! Darius," answered Maria, weeping, "great trouble in the house! Good missus not have two hours to live!" At this instant Mrs. Surrey and little Anna, pale and trembling both of them, appeared on the threshold.

"Edward!" cried the young girl; "have you brought me my cousin Edward?"

No one answered.

"And my brother!"

Dr. Van Stetten now approached; a glance was enough to tell him the truth.

"Ah!" he said sadly, "the good news I wanted so much to restore my poor patient to life has not come; but, on the contrary, here is another case for me, a grief for all."

They hastened to attend to Palmer, while the negress carried off Anna, who was still unconscious. The next morning, the people in the village of New Drontheim learned that Edward, as we have related, was still in the orang's power, that Mrs. Palmer had died in the night, and that her husband himself was at the point of death.

CHAPTER XVII

Five years had elapsed since the events we have just related.

During this interval great changes had taken place in New Drontheim, and the colony appeared to be in a wonderfully prosperous state. Numerous buildings, indigo factories, sugar factories, and mills had spread over the whole valley, as if they had sprung out of the ground; the great forest that formerly surrounded the houses had retreated several miles, and cultivation had extended widely in every direction.

The great bombax was no longer in existence; the very spot where Edward and his nurse had been attacked by the tiger was covered with fields of pepper, rice, and sweet potatoes. The population of New Drontheim had increased threefold in this short period. It is true that it was still composed of that strange mixture of Chinese, Malays, Negroes and Europeans that we are already acquainted with, but the number of Europeans had increased in a greater proportion, and there were always some European ships at anchor in the river.

The means of defending the colony had also become more important. Instead of the poor dilapidated fort on the top of the rock at the entrance of the harbour, there were two fine batteries one on each side of the river, well kept and well guarded, capable of resisting a considerable force for some time. Old Major Grudmann, who had retired on his pension, had been succeeded by another Governor, a man full of activity and zeal, who was as friendly to Palmer's family as his predecessor had been.

In the midst of the general prosperity, Palmer's establishment had not ceased to flourish; his buildings looked larger and better cared for than they used to do; there were a greater number of workpeople, and his storehouses were hardly emptied by ships coming to Sumatra for cargoes of spices and woods for dyeing and cabinet-work than they were filled again, as if by magic, with all sorts of commodities for the next purchaser. The house looked as neat and gay as ever, the garden had lost none of its Chinese curiosities, neither its pagoda with gilded turrets, nor its bamboo bridges across the stream with the waterfall, nor its china elephants with flower-pots for trunks. A wise and beneficent authority seemed still to rule the house and secure the comfort and prosperity of its inhabitants.

This influence, however, was not that of Richard Palmer. The head of the family had no longer the will and energy requisite for such a task. Though he did not utterly sink under the effects of despair, yet, when he came to himself again, life seemed of little value. Bereaved of his wife and son, he became gloomy and taciturn. He did not trouble himself at all about his affairs, and cared for nothing but roaming about in the woods, where he frequently spent five or six days together. When he returned home after these long absences, he looked gaunt, famished, and spent with fatigue.

In her brother's stead, Mrs. Surrey, who had superintended the household affairs in Elizabeth's lifetime, now assumed the management of everything in which the interests of the family were involved. Anna gave her as much assistance as she could.

When Richard, after a long and painful illness, had recovered his health, thanks to the skill and devotion of Dr. Van Stetten, he sank at first, as we have said, almost into despair. However, a thought, which by degrees became a fixed idea, took possession of his mind: according to the prevalent reports of the manners and habits of orangs there was reason to hope that his son was still alive; he must therefore find him, rescue, or at least avenge him. Through brooding continually over this one subject, Richard became persuaded that he must devote himself entirely to this rescue or revenge; and, when he had once arrived at this determination, his health began to improve rapidly. Henceforth he had an object in life; he thought that in listening to the suggestions of his paternal love, he was obeying the voice of that poor mother, who was calling to him from her grave to seek and save the lost child. So, leaving the affairs of the house to his sister and niece, he set himself to find means of putting his project into execution. He could not bear the idea of employing strangers to help him in this work of deliverance; besides, the Malays, the only native race that had the vigour and courage necessary to assist him effectually, were ferocious, treacherous, and unruly. He determined therefore to depend only on himself. For this purpose he must give up his European habits, must harden himself to fatigue and privation, and expose himself to the dangers of an adventurous life in these uninhabited places—in a word, he must turn savage. This task, in his state of mind, did not appear to him beyond his strength, and he set himself to it resolutely as soon as his health was restored.

His first care was to improve himself in shooting, by acquiring the skill and the quick-sightedness that are indispensable to a hunter in these wild solitudes. After constant practice, he acquired an extraordinary skill in the use of a large and very good rifle, which he had procured at great expense. In his hands the weapon was capable of doing wonderful execution; the largest animals, such as the elephant and the horned rhinoceros, common enough in the uninhabited parts of Sumatra, had fallen more than once under his fire. He had learned, too, to use the *kris* dexterously; and in deadly struggle with the monsters of the primeval forest he never failed to plunge the terrible blade exactly in the place where the blow would be fatal.

This was much, but it was not all; according to the programme he had laid down for himself, he must harden his body to the inclemency of that unhealthy climate; must accustom himself to do without the comforts of civilized life, and to sleep on the bare ground; he must try to improve to the utmost his sight and hearing, and this result could only be arrived at by long and persevering practice. So, during the five years that had elapsed, he had wandered about incessantly in the woods, living on the produce of his hunting, sleeping wherever night overtook him, and encountering with eagerness difficulties, toils, and dangers.

Thanks to this new education, Richard gradually became all he desired. His health was re-established, his limbs had acquired vigour and agility; and, although he had become much thinner, he could bear hunger, thirst and fatigue for a long time together. He could hear, at a considerable distance, the noise of steps on dry leaves; in the midst of the thickest underwood he could spy out the retreat of a wild beast, and in following a track several miles he had the marvellous instinct of the Red Indians of North America.

One could easily understand that Richard, in his long expeditions through the Sumatran forests, was exposed to very terrible adventures. Once he had to fight an enormous bear without any other weapon than the hatchet with which he was cutting his way through the underwood. Another time he found himself suddenly enveloped in the folds of a monstrous boa, that was dragging him away to crush him against a tree, according to the custom of these immense reptiles; but the planter, using with wonderful coolness the tactics of the Malays, drew his *kris*, cut the cold, slimy ring that encircled him, and then put an end to the snake by a shot from his rifle. We say nothing of the furious buffaloes that he brought to the ground with a ball in the middle of their foreheads, when they were rushing wildly upon him; of the tigers that he struck down at the moment when, stealing through the long grass to spring upon him, he could only see their shining eyes. But the danger he would have encountered most readily was precisely that which he had not the least occasion to brave; we mean an encounter with orangs. This species of ape is rare, and during this long period Palmer had only seen a few, and they were always at a great distance; but, ever active and alert, he looked to Providence to give him the opportunity he so earnestly desired. As to his son, in spite of his constant search, he had never found any trace of him, and everything led him to suppose that, if Edward was still living, the orangs had carried him away with them to some remote part of the forest to which he had not yet penetrated.

It remains for us to mention Palmer's companion in his hazardous expeditions, a dog named Robin. This Robin, which Richard had trained himself with the greatest care, was not a powerful animal, capable of using his teeth in his master's defence, like Boa's dog; on the contrary, it was a little animal, very much like the pug-dogs that are the delight of some old maids. Robin would be of no use in a serious conflict with the inhabitants of the forest; but, on the other hand, his hearing and scent were singularly fine, and he was constantly on the watch. During the day, when they were walking, Robin would go along as a scout, twenty paces in front of Richard, examining the bushes, smelling the tracks, and noticing everything that seemed suspicious to him. If any danger threatened, the dog immediately beat a retreat, with his tail between his legs, and uttering a low, timid bark, every variation of which his master had learned to know.

At night Richard would sometimes build a shelter for himself of branches; but frequently he slept in a recess in the rock, or in a hollow tree. Robin always had his place at his feet. Although apparently sound asleep, he would raise his head at the slightest sound, and give the usual signal. Richard was on his feet in a moment, with his rifle in his hand. In this way neither master nor dog could be taken by surprise, an incalculable advantage in these solitudes, where danger always comes unexpectedly, and is the more fatal in proportion as it is unforeseen.

Such was the changed man who had undertaken to find the lost child; such were the means of defence he possessed against the thousand dangers of this terrible kind of life. Nevertheless, he did not hide from himself that, in spite of his precautions, he would probably, sooner or later, fall a victim to his temerity. But this probability scarcely disturbed him: long since he had made the sacrifice of his life; and when the thought of one day becoming a prey to wild beasts presented itself to his mind, he would say, with gloomy resignation:

"Be it so! then my troubles will be ended."

Since the loss of Edward, five years, as we have said, had passed away, when Palmer set out on an excursion that took several days, and the results of which filled him with hope. He had left the house equipped as usual, carrying his "weapons, his hatchet, and some provisions. This time he resolved to explore a new part of the forest. It may be remembered that, at the time of his first expedition in company with Boa and Elephant-Slayer, an immense marsh of unknown extent, but which formed an insuperable obstacle in that direction, had compelled them to turn back. Since that time Palmer had examined minutely the part of the wood that lay between the marsh and the colony; but the morass, with its gigantic reeds sharp as sabres, with its slimy bottom swarming with crocodiles, with its pools of stagnant water and poisonous exhalations, had always stopped his way.

However, Palmer, in one of his previous rounds, had climbed a tall tree, and had thought he could distinguish, about the centre of this marsh, a narrow chain of rocks which might serve as a bridge across it, and it was at this point that he intended to try and cross.

In order to reach this spot he walked for two days. He guided himself by a little pocket compass, which he never went without, and by certain points that had become familiar to him. He also frequently consulted a kind of map of the country which he had traced himself, and on which he had carefully noted his previous discoveries. By the help of these marks he found the place he wanted without any difficulty, and this piece of success was soon followed by another. He was not mistaken in his anticipations: the basaltic rocks that he had perceived in the distance were continued in an irregular manner, but without intermission, across the marsh. It was a natural bridge which made it possible to cross these morasses, so dangerous in themselves and so perilously infested. Richard availed himself of it without troubling himself about a few gavials (crocodiles) that seemed disposed to dispute his passage, and soon entered a part of the forest perfectly new to him, and two or three times more extensive than that with which he was already acquainted. For the first time since his troubles a feeling something like joy awoke in his heart. Perhaps his son was concealed in this mysterious district; perhaps he should at last get at these invisible orangs, and punish the thief that had stolen Edward. However, in spite of his impatience to begin the search, he felt the necessity of not penetrating into this unknown land without having first discovered exactly where he was, in order that he might avoid doubts and fatal mistakes for the future. He chose as landmarks two or three high mountains in the centre of the island, noted down on his map several important observations, and then, and not till then, he dared to venture into those solitary places, where perhaps no human creature had ever penetrated since the creation.

This part of the country wore a very different aspect from that of the district on the other side of the marsh, and the hunter noticed, not without lively satisfaction, that it was suited in every particular for the abode of orangs. He knew, in fact, that these quadrumans are extremely susceptible of cold, and that in Sumatra, where the temperature is subject to sudden changes, especially in the neighbourhood of the mountains, they generally establish their dwellings in low, covered regions, sheltered from the wind. Now this part seemed exactly suited to the requirements of orangs. It was a kind of valley, or rather an extensive depression of the land, which extended as far as one could see. The trees, of colossal proportions, were no longer so very close to each other, but disposed in clumps in a picturesque manner. The ground was soft, without being marshy. The high grass formed a wavy sea of verdure, from which the venerable trunks of the bombax and palm-trees emerged. The landscape had the majestic and grand appearance of an American savannah.

Richard plunged resolutely into the high grass. After the first few steps all this brilliant picture disappeared from his sight, and he could see nothing but the tops of the nearest trees. Robin followed him, his nose in the air and his eye on the watch.

The planter was not long in discovering that this grand vegetation, apparently so quiet, was peopled by numerous inhabitants. Every minute clouds of birds—white spoonbills, rose-coloured flamingoes, herons with flowing crests—flew around him, and wide tracks in the prairie betrayed the customary paths of large quadrupeds; but, except a buffalo, which he found ruminating at the foot of a tuft of rattans, and which just turned towards him his melancholy eye, without disturbing himself, he saw no cause for alarm.

Palmer frequently met with pools of water, formed during the last rainy season, and which obliged him sometimes to go a long way round. In spite of these obstacles, in spite of the caution with which he was obliged to proceed, he made rapid progress, and had penetrated some way into the valley, when he perceived that the sun was about to set. Now he could not, without exposing himself to certain danger, spend the night in the open air, as he had done several times before, and it was time to think of a shelter for the night. Unfortunately he could see neither rock nor hollow tree there that would serve him for a temporary retreat. He was in the middle of the savannah, and it would be the utmost imprudence to wait till morning in the place where he was.

Palmer therefore set to work to discover a more favourable spot to establish his camp. He wished particularly to discover some running water, for not having ventured to quench his thirst at the pools of impure water he had met with on his way, he was almost dying with thirst, and his little companion was in the same condition. His desire was soon gratified, and he found a fresh, limpid stream, where both master and dog could drink at their leisure.

In other respects the place was such as could be wished for a resting-place during the night. Besides drinkable water—one of the first necessaries in these solitudes—there were cocoanut-trees, fig-trees, and bananas, loaded with fruit; and, what was more, Palmer spied out a hollow place among the gigantic roots of a banyan-tree, deep enough to serve as a shelter both for himself and Robin. After having made sure that this cavity was not already in the possession of certain inhabitants that would not willingly have consented to share it with him, he hastened to gather together moss and dry leaves to make a bed.

CHAPTER XVIII

While Palmer was thus occupied, a faint howl, which was all the sound that Robin was ever known to produce, for Robin never barked, attracted his attention. Although the hunter did not recognise the tone which told of imminent danger, he quickly raised his rifle to his shoulder and looked about to see if he could discover the reason for this warning. In a few minutes a little stag, of a kind very common in Sumatra, made its way out of the grass about twenty paces from him. Whether it was that he did not see Richard, or whether he was still ignorant that he had anything to fear from human beings, he walked on with a quiet step, and, rearing his majestic horns, he approached the rivulet without fear. He would be an easy prey, and the planter thought a cutlet of deer roasted in the ashes would be a nice supper for him and his dog after the fatigues of the day. He was on the point then of pulling the trigger of his rifle, and of disturbing the deep silence of the forest by firing, when Robin gave a second howl, but this time in a plaintive tone, very different from the first. The master recognised the signal of alarm, and thought no more of the poor stag, which, after having quenched his thirst, went away without guessing the danger he had just escaped.

Palmer stood still with his weapon at his shoulder, and looked in vain in all directions; he could hear no noise, and could see nothing. At last, tired with waiting, he turned to Robin to scold him for his mistake, and then he noticed that the dog, instead of troubling himself about what might be happening on the ground, had his eyes fixed on a tree about thirty or forty feet off. The planter then directed his attention to the same point, and at last distinguished some great body moving in the thickest part of the foliage: it was an orang.

Palmer's first impulse was to fire at this member of the detested race, but he thought better of it. The orang had not seen him, and did not seem uneasy. No doubt he lived somewhere near, and instead of killing him on the spot, to satisfy his blind revenge, would it not be better to follow him and watch his actions, ready to send a ball into him, if circumstances required it?

Richard lowered his gun for the second time, and throwing himself down behind a group of bamboos, continued to watch the orang.

The latter, as we have said, seemed to have no idea of danger, and probably little suspected the presence of an enemy in that part of the forest over which he had reigned as king till that day. He passed rather heavily from one tree to another. The slowness of his movements was easily accounted for; his hands were laden with figs and bananas, which he had just gathered from the neighbouring trees. It would not do, however, to trust too much to this apparent indolence. Palmer knew that at the least alarm the orang would quickly throw down his burden and disappear with the rapidity of thought.

When the orang had gone some little distance, the hunter seized Robin, fearing he might prove a serious trouble to him, and placed him in the hollow where he intended to sleep, ordering him to remain quiet. This was enough; the little creature, accustomed for a long time to such proceeding, crouched down in the cavity, and would not have thought of stirring all night without his master's leave.

Palmer, easy on this point, began to creep through the high grass, and was not long in discovering the orang, who was quietly continuing his course from tree to tree. The planter took the greatest pains not to be seen; but, unfortunately, the flocks of birds that flew away as he proceeded might betray him. Once even, he threw himself flat on the ground, thinking he was discovered. The orang, in fact, had come to a full stop on a thick branch, and had uttered a dull, guttural kind of noise. Was it a cry of alarm, or was it a call?

Palmer, both surprised and uneasy, did not know what to think, when the same noise was repeated a little further off, as if by an echo. Richard's joy at becoming certain of this was unutterable. His dearest wish was on the point of being realised; he was about to find what he had sought for in vain for five years—a colony of orangs!

In a few minutes he reached a glade, well sheltered from the wind by thick masses of trees, and traversed by the stream of which we have spoken. In this kind of enclosure the grass was worn, and looked as if it had been trodden under foot; on the bank of the stream a well-beaten, damp path led him to think that it was habitually used by some animals when they went to get water. But what struck the hunter at first was the sight of three huts almost exactly like those he had seen in the forest in his first expedition. Two of them were perched on the principal branches of an old ebony tree; the third was built against the trunk of a bombax-tree, a little apart. The latter, more spacious and infinitely better built than the others, was covered with palm-leaves that were still fresh, and it appeared greatly preferable to the miserable huts which afford shelter to some of the aboriginal inhabitants of the South Sea.

No orang was to be seen near these singular dwellings, and Richard doubted if they were still inhabited, but his uncertainty did not last long. The orang that had been his guide thither, when he had reached the glade, repeated his mysterious sound. Immediately something stirred in one of the huts in the ebony-tree, and two hideous heads—one large, with the prominent face of a beast, the other much smaller, and more like the human countenance—appeared at the entrance; then the two orangs came out of their dwelling, and advanced to meet the first. They were evidently mother and son, no doubt the wife and child of the one that was coming home with a store of provisions. Indeed, when they met, the greatest friendship seemed to exist between the three; the odd sounds began again; they sat down on a thick branch, and began to make their supper together on the fruits that the father had brought.

Palmer could now observe the strange creatures more closely than he had done till then. The father and mother were about six feet high; they were covered with brown hair, soft and silky, except the face, hands, and some other parts of the body that were bare and copper-coloured. They had hair on their heads and a moustache over the mouth, which was large, with thin tight lips. They had thick eyebrows, and their eyes had much vivacity and expression. There was something sedate and thoughtful in their way of moving, not commonly observed in any other kind of monkey. The little one looked lively, and almost intelligent, and seemed as if he showed signs of a certain capacity for education.

It is well known that young orangs that have been brought to Europe have shown a wonderful facility in imitating the different acts of men; and a modern savant has given an account of the wonderful feats attributed to a young female orang, which was presented to the Empress Josephine, and which Napoleon I. named *Mademoiselle Desbois*.

Richard was not in a humour to study the problem in natural history that the curious creatures offer, and which perhaps will remain unsolved for a long time. If, indeed, he had not feared compromising by too great precipitation the result of his discovery, he would have yielded to the temptation of disturbing this family meeting by discharging his rifle at them. But he put a restraint on himself, and his caution did not long remain unrewarded.

The youngest orang, while playing with a fine cocoa-nut that his father had brought, uttered two or three peculiar cries, and leaned down towards the hut at the foot of the tree. A voice from within answered him, and then a strange creature came out, whose form was altogether different from that of the orangs, and sent a thrill through the heart of the observer.

In truth, it was not an orang, let us say at once: it was a man, or rather a youth, who looked as tall and strong as a man.

His long tangled hair served him for clothing, and his body, although burnt by the sun, and hardened by contact with the air, showed indelible signs that he belonged to the white race. His nails were long and sharp, his movements sudden and agile; yet he had a look of gentleness, and even of wild melancholy, that inspired compassion.

We can give no idea of the ecstasy that Richard felt at this apparition. This miserable and degraded being was his son, his Edward.

No doubt there was a great difference between the fair rosy child that he had lost and this robust, sunburnt youth, who had sunk into a mere savage. However, Palmer could not be deceived; his paternal heart leapt within him. Forgetting everything else, he was on the point of raising himself above the high grass that concealed him; he was on the point of crying out "Edward! my dear Edward!" but the sounds died away on his lips, the arm on which he was resting bent under the weight of his body, and he fell with his face to the ground, unable to see, hear, or move. This momentary weakness had a happy result, for it gave time for him to think a little, and moderate these first transports.

When he came to himself, he felt the necessity of acting with extreme prudence, if he wished to restore the unhappy child he had just found to civilized life. He could not be sure of killing with a single ball the orang he had first perceived, and which he suspected was the one that had run away with Edward; besides, if he killed the head of the family, would not the female endeavour to avenge his death, as well as the young one, which seemed to be a formidable animal already?

There might be other orangs in the neighbourhood that would run thither at the first signal of alarm—how would Richard, in spite of all his courage and weapons, be able to defend himself against a troop of these animals, with whose indomitable vigour he was well acquainted? Again, and above all, how could he tell that the poor child, who had fallen into such a state of degradation, would recognise his father, and not rather take to flight when he saw him, or even try to defend himself from him? It would be better then to remain concealed, and wait for a favourable opportunity to act.

While the hunter thus found himself condemned for a time to inaction, the inhabitant of the hut advanced in a listless way towards the ebony-tree, on which the family had assembled. On seeing him, the young orang displayed the greatest joy; he redoubled his cries in a peculiar tone, and seemed to invite the youth to mount, by showing him the beautiful fruit he had in his hand. As Edward—for so we shall now call him—did not seem in a hurry to accept this invitation, he came down himself, hanging by his hands to the lowest branch of the tree; then, running on his two feet in rather an awkward manner, he threw himself on Edward's neck, whom he seemed very fond of, and gave him many hearty kisses, putting his lips to his cheeks and chest.

Edward, after having yielded in an absent way to the caresses of the young orang, freed himself from his embraces and passed on. But this was not what his companion wanted, and when he saw him going away he began to utter piercing cries, and dashed away from him the fruit that he had in his hand.

But as these demonstrations did not produce the desired effect, he put himself into a temper, and set to work to stamp, and then throwing himself on the ground, he began to cry, wiping away his tears with his fists, as children do sometimes.

This grief and anger did not affect Edward much, and he only smiled faintly. He kept on his way to the stream, bent down and drank out of the hollow of his hand: and after this he seemed to be hunting among the trees for something that would do for his evening meal. Spying out a large fig-tree loaded with fruit, he took hold of it in a determined way, and, with an agility little inferior to that of the orangs themselves, climbed to the top; there he took his seat on a branch, and began to eat his supper.

However, the mother seemed excited by the lamentations of her child; she made a great noise to appease him. Not being able to succeed in doing so, she came down to the ground, took him in her arms, and overwhelmed him with caresses; but nothing would do. As the little orang continued to weep and cry, she had recourse to a few gentle taps with her large hand to impose silence on her offspring.

Meanwhile the father, having finished his supper, had stretched himself out listlessly on a branch, a favourite attitude with orangs. However, he did not lose sight of Edward, who had gone too far away to please him. At last, finding that the youth was certainly too far off, or was too long returning, he roused himself from his indolence and went after him, springing from tree to tree, till poor Edward saw him coming, and no doubt fearing some violence, he hastened to fill his mouth with fruit, and let himself down the tree. Then he returned sadly towards the huts through the grass on the ground, while the orang, apparently satisfied with his docility, returned along the branches of the trees.

Palmer was cut to the heart to see his son and the son of his dear Elizabeth, the child of so many hopes, reduced to this condition of misery, that he was the slave of these hideous apes. And there was no longer any room to doubt that Edward was retained by force, and that the orangs exercised a constant watch over him, to prevent him from recovering his liberty, though it was clear he would not know what to do if he did get free, and this circumstance required the most serious attention. Edward and the quadruman family seemed now to be on very good terms. As soon as the youth approached, the little orang sprang into his arms, and covered him a second time with kisses. A fine fig that Edward gave him quite reestablished their friendship, and they played together on the grass for a little time with mutual pleasure.

The father resumed his careless attitude on the tree. As to the mother, seated at the foot of the tree, she watched their games; perhaps she felt some jealousy at the affection her son showed for the prisoner, but she only manifested it by uttering a few guttural sounds that did not seem to have any threatening character about them.

The planter observed all this with as much astonishment as grief; it seemed to him that Edward, though he had almost acquired a man's stature and strength during the last five years, had yet less intelligence than when he was a child. But he was soon obliged to leave his observations, and the reflections they suggested; the sun had set, the night was coming on, as usual, without being preceded by any twilight, and the sky had grown suddenly dark. In a little time the male orang repeated his grunting sound, and went into one of the huts on the ebony-tree, while the mother and child went into the other. Edward, on his part, hastened to his leafy abode, and everything became silent and still in the glade.

Richard knew not what to do, but he had an intense desire to try at once to get at his son in some way. While he was considering the subject, a terrible doubt flashed across his mind. During the preceding scenes Edward had not pronounced a single word; could it be that he had completely forgotten how to speak human language, and that he would be unable to understand and answer when anyone spoke to him? Then what circumspection would be necessary if the powers of his mind had been thus lessened by the solitude, silence, and society of brute creatures? In spite of all this the poor father determined to risk an attempt at once.

After having given the orangs time to fall asleep, and being quite sure that it was too dark to be seen, he crept to Edward's hut, crouched down behind the wall of foliage opposite the entrance, and in English, as the language that used to be most familiar to the child, he said, in a gentle voice:

"Edward, dear Edward! do you still think of your father?"

There was a sudden movement in the hut, as if someone got up from his seat; at the same time Palmer heard a sound of gasping for breath that betrayed unusual emotion. Perhaps the dweller in the cabin thought himself the plaything of a dream, when Richard, after a short pause, continued in the same tone, stopping between each word:

"Edward! Edward! have you forgotten your father who loved you so dearly, and your mother, and your cousin Anna?"

Hardly had he finished these words than he was frightened himself at their effect. Whether the human voice which he had not heard for so long struck him with terror, or whether he understood the meaning of these words, Edward seemed seized with a strange kind of frenzy. He rushed out of his house uttering frightful cries, and began to run up and down in a frantic way. In his hand he brandished a club, and beat the air with it as if he were striking at a phantom.

As he ran he continued to utter wild piercing shrieks which had nothing human about them. At last, desperate, breathless, and streaming with perspiration, he threw down his stick, seized the trunk of a tree, climbed it in a minute, and disappeared among the branches.

Palmer was astounded at the result of his experiment; he waited for a long time without seeing Edward return; much discouraged, he returned to the place where he meant to spend the night, and found Robin still in the hollow where he had left him. The little animal was dying with hunger, and his master hastened to give him some supper. As for himself, he did not dream of eating, in spite of the fatigues of the day. He did not dare light a fire, as he generally did, to scare away the wild beasts, for the bright light would certainly alarm the orangs, and perhaps his son himself. Besides, he had no wish to go to sleep, and he could depend on himself to keep watch during the rest of the night. So he settled himself in his poor lodging, and with his rifle on his knees, began to think over the difficulties of his situation.

It was not enough indeed to have found Edward—he must get

him away at once from the power of these formidable creatures; and Richard knew well enough what they were capable of to appreciate the danger of such an enterprise. In order to gain his object it would be necessary to hold some communication with Edward, and to arrange a way of escape with him; but how could he arrange anything with him when the very sound of the human voice produced such an effect on the young savage?

Now that Richard had found his son, he did not want to run the risk of losing him again by taking any imprudent step, or one of which the success was uncertain. So, after having thought a long time, he decided on the following plan: not to attempt anything at present, but to return to the colony for help; to come back again quickly with a large number of men, who would surround Edward's hut and take possession of him in spite of any resistance the orangs might make. This plan would require some little time to put into execution, and would compel the father to leave the child for some days still in his miserable condition; but it was the safest one, and Palmer would not try any other.

Still one subject of anxiety tormented him; what had become of Edward? In his blind terror had he not hurt himself seriously by running against the trees and rocks? This thought worried the hunter during the rest of the night. Several times he was on the point of going back to the hut to see if his son had returned, but it was advisable, in order to ensure the success of his plan, that nothing should disturb the serenity of the orangs, and the other animals of that genus, which, during his absence, might quit their present dwelling and go and establish themselves in another part of the forest. However, not being able to overcome his uneasiness, he glided to a mass of underwood whence it was easy for him to watch the inhabitants of the glade; he settled himself there with Robin, and waited impatiently for day.

Day came at last, and the brightness of early morning lighted up the woods. Unfortunately the pestilential *cabout* rolled in heavy waves under the overhanging trees and made it impossible to see at any distance. It was useless to hope that the fog would pass off for some hours, and the hunter, who was in a hurry to be up and doing, had no time to lose in making observations. But he considered that if this vexatious mist prevented him from seeing, it; must also prevent him from being seen, and he went nearer the huts, taking advantage of every inequality of the ground to conceal himself.

He soon had the satisfaction of seeing Edward return with slow steps to his cabin. The poor boy looked even more downcast and sad than the evening before, as if the event of the previous day had awakened some bitter remembrances. With head bent down, he passed close by his father, and went and sat down before his hut in a gloomy, dreamy way.

Palmer guessed, or thought he guessed, what was disturbing his weak mind: and what would he not have given to run into his son's arms, to quiet him, and explain what appeared dark and terrible to him? But his first attempt had succeeded too ill for it to be prudent to risk another, and the father shed tears as he was obliged to content himself with murmuring:

"Ah, poor child, take courage! a few days more and your sufferings will be at an end!" Palmer then began to make his retreat with the greatest caution. Having warned the dog by a sign that he must be silent, he set to work to creep slowly through the brushwood, and in a short time they found themselves out of the glade.

CHAPTER XIX

It was not without a pang that the father turned away from his beloved child, whom he had found again after incurring so much difficulty and danger on his behalf. When he caught his last glimpse of Edward through the mist, he was still sitting before his hut plunged in a sad reverie. He was resting his head on his hand, and his long tangled hair formed a veil to his grief, but this veil was not thick enough to hide the great tears that chased each other down his sunburnt cheeks.

Palmer set off at a quick rate. He reckoned that in two days he could traverse the distance, which was considerable, that lay between him and New Drontheim, and return on the third with a numerous company to effect his son's deliverance.

But, in spite of the precautions he had taken, and the points that he was quite sure about, he lost his way more than one in the savannah. After having recrossed the winding ridge of rocks that extended across the marshes, he hoped that his progress would be more rapid, but an unfortunate accident again delayed the fulfilment of all his anticipations.

Little Robin, as he ran hither and thither round his master, to make sure of the road, was bitten by one of those venomous reptiles that infest the forests of Malaysia. Such an accident was nothing new; and twenty times over, by applying herbs that he was acquainted with, to this faithful servant's wound, Palmer had succeeded in curing him very speedily. Now he hastened to apply his usual remedy to the place, but the result did not answer his expectation. The dog continued to suffer, and swelled up to an immense size; he was soon unable to walk, and Palmer was obliged to stop and attend to him. But all his efforts were useless; the poor creature expired, gazing at his master with a look full of affection, and licking his hands.

His sudden death grieved the hunter very much, and made him feel very downcast.

"Dear little companion of my sufferings and miseries," he said, with tears in his eyes, laying down the lifeless body, "did you think, then, that I should not want you any more? Why did you leave our task unfinished?"

He did not like the body to become the prey of wild beasts, and dug a little grave for it with his *kris*; then he set off again with a sore heart.

This event lost him some precious time. Besides, being deprived of the help of Robin's wonderful instinct, he could not proceed with so much rapidity and assurance as before. So, instead of reaching the colony the next day, as he had wished to do, he did not arrive till the third day.

When he reached the house, the new Governor, Mr. Deursen, was paying a visit and chatting with Mrs. Surrey and Anna. The Governor was surprised at Palmer's condition. Edward's father was looking old and worn, though at times he manifested extraordinary vigour. His face was bronzed and wrinkled; his long, matted beard showed how little he cared about his own appearance, and there was a kind of wildness at times in his sunken eye. His dress corresponded with his countenance. He who once dressed with so much care, when he wished to please a beloved wife, was clothed in skins, which were only half tanned, and fastened round his limbs with leathern thongs. These substantial garments had, however, suffered from the thorns and sharp grass, for in several places they left his hard, dry, hairy skin exposed, which neither the stings of insects nor the thorns of the bushes could penetrate.

Though Palmer was generally overcome with fatigue when he returned from his expeditions into the interior of the country, he had never seemed so reduced as he did now. His feet were bleeding, he could not stand upright, and his feverish look led them to guess that to all his other sufferings was added that of hunger.

However, on perceiving his sister and niece, he quickened his speed, and waved his arm as if he was impatient to announce some great news. At last, when he reached them, he cried out, in a hollow voice:

"Sister Anna, there's no doubt!—he is living, I have *seen him*!"

He stopped, and leaned against the door-post, for his strength failed him, and he turned giddy.

"Richard," asked Mrs. Surrey, "what do you mean? whom are you talking about?"

"Uncle," cried Anna, in her turn, "what has happened?"

He tried to answer, but the sounds died away on his lips, his head swam round, and his legs gave way under him. However, he murmured at last, with a great effort:

"Edward!—Edward!—Edward!"

And he fell down insensible.

When he came to himself, thanks to the care lavishly bestowed on him by Van Stetten, who arrived at that very minute, he pressed the doctor's hand, and cried:

"Yes, sister,—yes, dear Anna,—yes, my friends, Edward is

living; I have seen him; I have been within a few paces of him; I could have talked with him if he had been able to recognise my voice, and understand and answer me."

And he related in detail the incidents of his last expedition into the deep forest. All present listened with an air of dumb amazement. Every now and then Mrs. Surrey and Anna uttered exclamations of terror, or, raising their clasped hands to heaven, shed abundant tears.

When Palmer had finished his tale, the Governor seemed very thoughtful.

"I have heard wonderful stories told of the great apes of Africa and Malaysia," he answered; "but really, Mr. Palmer, if anyone but you had told me such things I should not have believed him. However, your son is alive still, and that is the great thing. We may save him, and; though he is reduced to such a deplorable condition, restore him to civilized life. He is young; education will efface the traces of his present degradation; and why should he not again become the pride and joy of his family? Mr. Palmer, do you intend to be long before you attempt the rescue of the poor child?"

Palmer answered in a firm tone:

"I shall set out to-morrow morning."

Anna and Mrs. Surrey tried to reason with him; he would not even give them time to open their mouths.

"You are going to talk to me of the fatigue I have just had," he replied, in a peremptory tone; "say no more about it! I am quite rested; I feel quite strong and ready to start again. If I were not obliged to make some positively necessary preparations, and to collect a sufficient number of men to secure the success of my enterprise, I should set off at once."

The poor women, quite abashed, dared not say another word.

"I understand your impatience, Mr. Palmer," answered the Governor, "and I share it. You have need, you say, of a great number of men to carry out your plan effectively; I can get you some. In the roads there are some Lascars that we took in at Malacca to look after the rigging; they are iron men, accustomed to tiger-hunting in impenetrable jungles, and hardened to all the fatigue of life in the woods. We will have, too, any natives whom you can persuade to come, and I intend to accompany you myself. How long do you think this excursion into the forest will take?"

"Three or four days at most."

"Then it is settled, Mr. Palmer; I will go with you."

"We shall succeed!" cried Palmer. "We shall find Edward; and get him away from these horrible creatures that have got him in their power. In a few days I am sure he will become as gentle, kind, and affectionate, as he used to be when he was a baby."

The Governor sent for several Lascars, and told them what he expected of them, promising them a handsome reward, which they were by no means disposed to refuse.

They were charmed, moreover, at the idea of wandering about for some days in the woods. So they consented in the name of their absent comrades, and set to work to consider how they could let them know, that they might all be ready at the appointed hour for setting out.

On their part Elephant Slayer and the other Malays, knowing Palmer's generosity, and being sure of a handsome reward, declared they would willingly join the expedition.

Next morning, a little before daylight, as Richard had desired, all who were to take part in the expedition, including the faithful Darius, met in the court of the house. Though it was not very dark, the *cabout* rendered the use of lights necessary, and several torches fixed in the ground shed a reddish light around them. The Lascars and Malays were already at the place of rendezvous, some dressed in their long white garments, others wrapt in their large *sarongs*, as the morning air was fresh, but all of them wore, under these flowing robes, a very simple costume which could not get in their way in the midst of the inextricable underwood of the forest. They were provided with cutlasses and hatchets to cut a passage for themselves through the thickets, and besides they had heavy guns and some of the long match locks which are still used in these barbarous countries. The Malays would have liked to have furnished themselves with their ordinary weapons-poisoned arrows—but Palmer set himself against the very idea of it, for fear, if any scuffle took place, his son might receive some mortal wound; and they were obliged to submit to his orders.

However, the two races formed distinct groups; whether it was that the difference of their language kept them apart, or that they had a feeling of distrust to each other, they remained at the opposite ends of the court without holding any communication with one another. The two groups consisted in all of about forty hunters, and this number seemed more than sufficient for the success of the enterprise.

Richard Palmer superintended everything. Though he had had hardly two hours rest during the preceding night, he seemed full of courage and vigour. Dressed in his leathern costume, which was much faded by the sun and torn by the thorns, he went about from one to another, busying himself about the smallest details.

Many people, too, were moving about the court, and the lights, which could be seen incessantly passing and repassing the windows of the house, showed that the people indoors were as busy as those out-of-doors.

In a little time fresh torches were seen in the avenue, shining through the mist, giving warning of the approach of a second band of hunters; it was the Governor and some other persons.

Deursen was already equipped for an expedition into the woods; he wore long gaiters, deer-skin breeches, a hunting jacket trimmed with light gold lace, and a very low hat. A well-armed negro followed him, to carry his rifle and the little baggage he could not dispense with.

Richard gave truce for a moment to his engrossing cares, and went forward to meet his guest. He shook hands cordially with the Governor.

"Mr. Palmer," said the latter, "I bring you a new comrade, whose assistance may perhaps not be useless to you."

And he pointed out Dr. Van Stetten.

"Thanks, my dear doctor," answered the planter; "you are welcome among us. Have you made your preparations?"

"Oh dear, yes," replied Van Stetten good-temperedly. "My case and a few necessary medicines are in the pockets of my coat, and I have not forgotten my parasol."

And he exhibited the big old umbrella that he generally took with him on his walks.

The hunters filed off down the avenue by the light of torches.

As day began to dawn they arrived at the edge of the forest. When the clumps of tall trees became indistinctly visible in the mist, Palmer ordered a general halt. So far there had been no danger to fear, and each one could walk as he liked; but on quitting the inhabited districts some precautions must be taken, if they wished to avoid danger and confusion.

The planter now intended to establish strict discipline among the band of men, and made it a rule that no one should wander away during the course of the journey. He himself, as guide and chief of the expedition, proposed to walk first with a few men armed with hatchets and knives to clear a path if necessary. Within reach of this advanced guard, a certain number of hunters were to hold themselves ready to repulse any attacks of wild beasts by firing at them. Behind them came Deursen, Doctor Van Stetten, and lastly the horse laden with baggage.

The rearguard consisted of the rest of the hunters. All the men were advised not to leave the ranks under any pretext whatever. A shot, followed directly by a shout, was to be the signal of alarm; all those who heard the signal were to run to the help of the comrade in danger. The sound of a horn that Palmer was to carry slung over his shoulder was to rally the whole troop in any case of pressing necessity.

Palmer gave his instructions in different languages, that they might be understood by all present, and Deursen himself repeated them to the Lascars. When they were quite sure that nobody would be able to plead ignorance of the rules, they set off marching in the order agreed upon, and entered the forest.

CHAPTER XX

It did not seem at first sight that so many precautions were necessary; the part of the wood they were traversing was frequented by the colonists, and here and there traces of paths were visible. But as they advanced the trees became thicker, the creepers more entangled, and the thorns and stems of the tree-ferns, aloes, and cactuses, more entwined.

But at the same time, Palmer, an experienced guide, chose with wonderful sagacity the places where the ground was most even, where the underwood was least dense, and if occasionally they had to plunge straight into thickets that seemed almost impenetrable, they more often walked under high trees where the ground, being covered with a thick, velvety carpet of moss, offered no obstacle to their progress, and allowed them to advance rapidly.

It was through a place of this kind that they passed about an hour after they had entered the forest. It was already broad daylight, though the mist and the thick foliage overhead prevented them from seeing the sun. It was deliciously cool in these shady places, and sparkling drops of dew hung from the leaves. The white costume of the Lascars, the drapery of the Malays, the shining weapons, the lively groups of men, formed a pleasing picture in the midst of these majestic woods. No other sound was heard than the strange songs of a few birds; no other inhabitants were to be seen than the great lizards that ran up and down the trunks of trees, which were covered with beautiful parasitic orchids, little bearded monkeys springing from branch to branch, or a few deer, which, starting up almost under the feet of the hunters, ran away down the long avenues which stretched away further than eye could see. However, the mist cleared off at last, and the sunbeams flashed through the forest trees here and there like fiery darts. A halt became necessary for the men, who had had frequently to use their hatchets in cutting a path through the thickets. So they stopped to rest during the extreme heat of the day.

Up to this point the journey had been made under the most favourable auspices. They had seen no wild beasts, the difficulties in their way did not appear to be insurmountable, and the heat, though very great, was not unbearable under the shade of the trees. So the travellers were as full of zeal and courage as they had been in the morning. It must be confessed that the Lascars and Malays still kept apart; but thus far they were equally obedient to the orders of their chiefs, and in spite of the dislikes and antipathies of the two races, the peace between them did not seem likely to be disturbed.

After two hours" rest they set off again. Palmer had decided that they should encamp that same evening on the border of the extensive morass that divided the forest in half, not far from the ridge of rocks recently discovered. He had calculated that by spending the night in this place it would be easy next day to cross the ridge, to reach the region of the orangs, and after having rescued Edward, to return and encamp in the same place. Thus the journey, occurred, would not occupy more said at first.

However, the second half of the journey was not so easily accomplished as the first. They plunged afresh into thickets where their progress was intercepted by numerous and ever-recurring obstacles. The character of the soil varied at every step; sometimes it was dry and pebbly, sometimes spongy and damp, but more frequently overrun with the rank and vigorous vegetation of tropical regions. No difficulty daunted the indefatigable Palmer; he was always at the head of the troop, guiding his companions without hesitation through these gloomy solitudes. By means of certain marks that he had traced on the trunks of certain trees he could discover at once towards what point he was proceeding, however confined his view might be.

Still, it was late when they reached the spot where they were to encamp for the night.

The character of the landscape was far grander than that of any landscape in our temperate zones. The marsh extended as far as the eye could reach, bordered by the irregular line of the forest, which was indistinctly visible on the other side in the misty distance. Here and there were large pools of leaden, stagnant water, and beds of reeds, which waved, with a metallic sound at the least breath of wind. Little islands of mud lay on the bosom of the sleeping waters, shaded by groups of bamboos, and willows with pale foliage, or banyans, or the sacred fig-trees, so common on the banks of the Ganges. A fiery sky hung over the gloomy scene, and in the air reddish mists floated low and heavy, which looked as if they must contain the seeds of disease and death. Now the sun, like a globe of red-hot iron, cast only oblique rays over the plain, and increased yet more the solemn sadness of this lonely spot. At this time of the evening, herons as white as snow, ibis with plumage as red as fire, snake-birds with curving necks, were flying about in great numbers over the lagoons, and uttering startling cries. In the distance were seen wild boars and tapirs, which, alarmed at the sight of men, hurried away from the neighbourhood of the marshes to their ordinary retreats in the depths of the forest. Monkeys, great and small, chased each other to the tops of the palm-trees, flying lizards sprang from branch to branch, supported by the large membranes of their scaly feet. The very reeds, to judge by their long undulations, seemed to be traversed by numerous reptiles, perhaps by the enormous boa, the sovereign of these pestilential spots. They began to hear the hoarse cry of the gigantic toad, peculiar to tropical countries. And lastly certain ripples in the liquid mud and certain black spots that appeared every now and then among the large leaves of the water-lilies, made them suspect that the crocodiles were beginning to stir at the bottom of the water, waiting till it was dark enough for them to come and sport on the banks.

Such was the spectacle, at once grand and imposing, that presented itself to the eyes of the hunters as they halted at the edge of the morass.

The men set to work at once to encamp. Scattered about under gigantic trees, so high that they were almost frightful to look at, they seemed like dwarfs, so small did they appear compared with the colossal proportions of everything around them. They had thrown off all useless clothing, in order to fulfil their task more easily, and they had no other clothing than a pair of drawers, which left exposed to view their black or copper-coloured bodies streaming with perspiration. Some of them cut down young trees, either for fires during the night or to supply materials for a hut for the leaders of the expedition. Others busied themselves with preparations for supper, and before long the wreaths of smoke, rising slowly into the air, pointed out the kitchen of the bivouac.

The sound of hatchets, the crash of falling trees, the cries of the men at work, and a few shots fired occasionally, were repeated with grand effect by the echoes of the primeval forest, where those different sounds soon died away, as into empty space.

In the middle of this general activity, a quarrel broke out between the Malays and Lascars. Several times they seemed on the point of fighting, and the Governor was obliged to put his hand on the pistols shining in his belt to induce them to abstain from more serious provocations than those of gesture and voice. This was how it happened.

All the morning, as we have seen, Malays and Hindoos had formed two distinct bands, who watched each other with distrust, if not with a feeling of hostility. The Malays, who were clever and experienced hunters, had succeeded during the day in killing two deer and a young boar, while the Lascars, either less skilful or less fortunate, had only knocked down a few birds. Now they had brought very few provisions with them; they had reckoned on the produce of the chase and the wild fruits of the forest for the support of this numerous company; it was, therefore, necessary to make an equal division of the food among all the travellers. Although the Hindoos in general abstain from meat, the warlike caste of the Lascars very willingly form an exception to this rule, and those belonging to this band of hunters, exhausted and famished, did not seem at all inclined just then to listen to the precepts of their religious faith. So they claimed their share of the tempting game, and it was this claim that offended the Malays. Whether the latter were actuated by a feeling of secret enmity, or simply yielded to their proud and quarrelsome dispositions, they refused to share the produce of the chase with the rest, and especially with the Hindoos. Insulting words were exchanged between the two parties, and they were becoming so excited that the leaders were obliged to interpose their authority to stop a conflict which might have had most serious consequences.

The night was by no means a quiet one. Myriads of mosquitoes filled the air as soon as the sun went down, and would not allow the tired travellers a moment's rest. Besides, in spite of the large fires which they kept up all night, they had several alarms from elephants and tigers. The tigers especially were very numerous and fierce; they roared incessantly round the camp, and their hoarse cries were echoed from every part of the forest. The inhabitants of the marshes were no quieter; not to speak of the giant toad, which croaked away among the reeds, a continual rattling was heard from the side of the lake, and a kind of roaring, like that of a pair of blacksmith's bellows. Sometimes, too, prodigious plunges occurred, as if heavy masses had fallen into the water: it was the crocodiles or gavials that were amusing themselves in their fashion. Several even were not content with this large lake for the theatre of their games. A Lascar on duty at the edge of the morass, having fallen asleep at his post, was awakened by the horrible putrid odour that these animals spread around them. He sprang to his feet, and perceived, by the light of the moon, a gavial, twelve or fifteen feet long, gliding up to him, and preparing to attack him; the Lascar fired a shot to frighten him away, and the gavial slowly retired. The sentinel, as may easily be imagined, did not have any more sleep for the rest of the night. The dawn came, however, with its usual accompaniment of thick mists; and as soon as it got light, the noises abroad changed their character. The elephants left off roaming about under the trees, the branches of which they broke with their trunks; the tigers were silent, and the gavials returned to their mud, and the songs of a thousand happy birds hailed the return of day. It was advisable that the band should take advantage of this cool time, the most agreeable in the day. So, at Palmer's call, they were all on foot in a few minutes. They rolled up the cloaks that had served for beds during the night, extinguished the fires, and breakfasted quickly on what remained of last night's provisions. Those of the travellers, Malays or Lascars, who were Mussulmans, went to the lake, and while some performed the ablutions prescribed by the Koran, the rest, turning towards Mecca, addressed their morning prayer to Allah.

Palmer was about to give the signal for departure, when Deursen said to him:

"Affairs do not go on very well between the Malays and Lascars, Mr. Palmer. There are comings and goings and whisperings among these people that make me suspicious. I am afraid that on the first opportunity it will be almost impossible to hinder a new collision."

"I have noticed the signs of quarrelling that you mention, Mr. Deursen," replied Palmer sadly. "I hope, however, our men will give us time to accomplish the task for which we came into these solitudes: to-morrow evening we shall be returning to New Drontheim, where the means of repression will not be wanting in case of open insubordination. From now till to-morrow the parties will probably have dangers and difficulties enough to put up with, to make them forget their mutual grievances. We must be on our guard, and by exercising at once firmness and address, we shall manage, no doubt, to keep the peace till the end of the journey."

The Governor, though he did not altogether share this hope, nodded as a sign of assent. Five minutes after the whole band set off and proceeded along the edge of the marsh to look for the ridge of rocks that formed a kind of natural bridge across it. The mist being thicker over the water than in the plain, it was impossible to distinguish any objects more than ten paces ahead, and the walking over this muddy ground was dangerous. Besides, in this fog, it was quite possible that they might miss the rather narrow path which led to the other part of the forest. Palmer himself, whose directions had always proved right, and whose observations had been found to be so correct, seemed now uncertain and hesitated. Happily the sun, as it increased in power, partly scattered this troublesome mist, and allowed the travellers to discover at last the path they were seeking.

It was, as we have said, an irregular line of rocks that in certain places hardly rose more than a few feet above the level of the lake; of these rocks some were bare and barren; others were covered with shrubs and brushwood: occasionally they were separated by pools of stagnant water. The whole chain, from its numerous windings, was four or five miles long, and the remains of the mist, by hiding the opposite side, added to its gloomy appearance.

Hardly had they set foot on the ridge than the travellers saw the necessity of helping one another. They were obliged to try the ground at each step, for the least carelessness might lead to a fatal fall. The horse frequently stuck in the mud, and it seemed impossible to make him proceed. Besides, all the monsters of this pestilential bog seemed to have undertaken to defend their domains against the invasion of man; and if they had not taken the precaution of firing every few minutes, terrible accidents would probably have occurred. Here, a boa-constrictor, surprised on his rock while he was lying digesting his food, withdrew majestically into the reeds.

Further on, an enormous crocodile, disturbed while he was sleeping in the sun, plunged into the water with a dismal snort, turning his mournful, prominent eye as he went on those who had the audacity to interfere with him. In every direction these loathsome creatures showed where they had been, by leaving clammy, fetid slime on the ground behind them. We need hardly mention the innumerable little snakes, lizards of every size, scorpions, millipedes, and centipedes, that swarmed round the travellers. As to birds, they frequently rose in swarms so thick and so clamorous that they inspired the hunters with more alarm than even the gavials and the boas.

Dr. Van Stetten, under the shelter of his voluminous umbrella, no longer wandered about to the right and left to gather rare plants or catch insects, but walked on with difficulty, overwhelmed by the insupportable heat.

However, thanks to Palmer's cautions and the perfect order he maintained among his men, the passage was performed without any accident. Long before the sun had half completed its course, the whole band reached the end of the ridge safe and sound, and halted under the shadow of some pandanus trees on the border of the savannah lately discovered by Palmer.

CHAPTER XXI

Here a new plan of proceeding became necessary. Useful as shouting, running, and firing had been in crossing the bog, now it was just as necessary to keep silence and glide along unperceived. They were close to the district frequented by the orangs, and they were well aware what a fine sense of hearing these animals possess. If the orangs were once put upon their guard, some of the adventurers might easily become their victims. Concealed among the foliage, they might, according to their wont, break the hunter's skull with their clubs before he had even guessed they were near. None of the men belonging to the band were ignorant of these facts, and the boldest felt the need of prudence as they entered the part of the forest inhabited by such creatures.

However, Palmer had decided to go by himself first and discover whether Edward was still in the neighbourhood. He invited his comrades, therefore, to rest in the place where they were. After having strongly advised Deursen and the doctor to see that the men were not thinking of taking advantage of this interval of leisure for any other purpose than rest, he plunged into the savannah, and soon disappeared in the long grass.

More than an hour passed away and he did not return. The sun was then in its greatest power; the heat was so overpowering that no human creature could brave it with impunity. So the Malays, negroes, and Lascars, in spite of their secret animosity, slept side by side. Deursen himself, who was lying on the grass, seemed completely knocked up. As to the doctor, stretched on his back, shaded by his old umbrella, he was looking perfectly unable to stir, and the large ants of the forest might have eaten him up on the spot for all the power he had to free himself from their torture. Everybody, however, soon came to life again when Palmer, issuing from out of the savannah at last, and running towards the sleepers, cried, in a trembling voice:

"I have seen Edward; I have seen the orangs! Get ready, everybody. We can reach them in half an hour."

As we have said, the men were on their feet in an instant. In some, the magic word, the orangs, drove away all wish to sleep: in others, the name of Edward recalled the object of the expedition, and the frightful disaster which they had to repair.

Van Stetten, who, after incredible efforts, had managed to get on his feet, said, as he wiped the perspiration from his forehead, and uttered deep sighs:

"Oh! if I have only an opportunity of measuring the facial

angle of an orang! The savants of Europe will never know what such a discovery has cost me."

Palmer gave his men most minute directions, in order to avoid committing any mistakes that might render the expedition abortive. It was agreed that the hunters should form a large circle round the place inhabited by the orangs, and that this circle should draw in gradually in perfect silence; that they should try above everything to secure Edward, and they were forbidden to fire at the orangs, except in a case of absolute necessity; for if one was killed or wounded, the others might inflict serious injuries on the party. Deursen was to go with his Lascars and occupy the post appointed for him by Palmer, while Palmer himself was to advance on the other side with the Malays; a few notes of the horn that the leader carried slung over his shoulder would give the signal for meeting.

"Now," continued Palmer, "let everybody be prudent and take care of himself; for, if the rescue of my son should cost the life of any of his deliverers, it would be a cause of deep regret to me, and hereafter to Edward himself."

In a few minutes the whole troop advanced and entered the savannah.

CHAPTER XXII

Palmer had his reasons for recommending his comrades to be extremely careful; in the little exploring excursion he had just made, he had discovered that the danger was greater than he had expected at first. This is what had happened to him. In the part of the wood he had been to, the trees, as we said before, were far apart; nevertheless, every time the planter passed under one of these trees, he examined the foliage carefully, to make sure that an orang on guard was not hidden in it. But at that time of day, when the heat was insupportable, all creation seemed quiet and dormant. Except a few snakes that fled away before Palmer, nothing stirred around him; the very insects were silent. The birds, which at his first appearance in this untrodden district flew away in every direction, now did not seem as if they could make up their minds to leave the long grass where they could still find a little moisture and coolness. As to Palmer, he appeared quite insensible to the influence of the extreme temperature and to the burning heat of the sun, which was so exactly over his head that his body cast no shadow. Not a drop of perspiration ran down his bony, sunburnt face. He breathed the burning air, which seemed as if it issued from a furnace, without difficulty. He thought of nothing but his son and the important scene that was about to be played in that very spot.

As he advanced with the greatest caution, he directed his steps towards the wooded part inhabited by the orangs. In a short time the trees around him became more numerous, closer to one another and thicker, and he had nearly reached the spot he was aiming at when a slight creaking was heard overhead. He stopped instantly, held his breath, and, after having silently cocked his rifle, examined the tree whence the sound proceeded. An orang was lying idly in a mass of orchids at a height of about twenty feet, and seemed to be enjoying his siesta; he had moved in his flowery bed and broken a branch, and thus attracted the planter's attention.

Palmer pointed his rifle at it for a few minutes. At the slightest hostile movement of the orang he would have touched the trigger. But the orang had not perceived the hunter, and, after a sonorous yawn, fell asleep again quietly. It did not enter into Palmer's plan to begin the attack immediately, for fear of disturbing the neighbouring colony. So, when he was quite sure that the sentry was sound asleep again, he went back quietly, to try and enter the glade on the other side.

Having made another turn, he began to creep through the grass, using the utmost care not to be discovered. This caution was not needless, for he again saw three or four orangs sitting together on the trees, in careless attitudes, while the huts themselves appeared to be occupied by their usual inhabitants.

Was this increase of the band accidental, or had Richard on his former visit only made acquaintance with part of the inhabitants of the glade? In any case, it added greatly to the difficulties of the enterprise. However, as may easily be imagined, the planter did not dream of retreating; he continued to creep through the underwood, and his bold perseverance was rewarded with success.

On the bank of the stream that crossed the glade were Edward and the young orang that seemed to be the usual companion of his games. They were both coming out of the water, where they had just been taking a bath, and Edward, to protect himself from the rays of the sun, had made a kind of garland of damp grass, and had rolled it round his naked body. The water dropped from his long hair and from this garment, which was graceful, though rather too primitive. Edward had no longer that gloomy, melancholy look which had struck his father at first; with a smile on his lips, he bore the teasing of his companion, who tormented him in a thousand different ways. However, the young orang, either intentionally or by accident, having pulled his hair, he turned round to avenge the insult; but the frolicsome quadruman had already gained a neighbouring tree, which he climbed with the greatest ease.

Edward wanted to do the same, but it was very plain that, in spite of his agility, he could not contend with his friend in this kind of exercise. He perceived it himself, for when he had climbed half-way up the tree, he came down again. Palmer noticed this little fact with pleasure; it proved at least that his poor boy would not be able to escape him by springing from tree to tree; and if they could succeed in surrounding him on the ground they might easily make sure of him. So he continued to watch him, hoping that by studying the habits of the savage he might find means to accomplish his projects of deliverance.

Edward, despairing of reaching his companion, or disdaining to avenge himself, had returned to the stream, while the young orang seemed to be setting him at defiance and laughing at him. Without troubling himself about him any more, he went to the foot of a willow, and taking up a bow and arrows that he had placed there, began to shoot at the trunk of a tree, for the sake of practice, it seemed. He never missed his aim; but the bow was not a very formidable one, and differed little from those given to children. The cord looked as if it was made of the fibre of the cocoa-nut-tree or of some other fibrous plant; the arrows, though made of very hard wood, were not tipped with any metal to make them sharp, and certainly could not hurt anything larger than a bird or small animal.

Edward seemed to take the greatest pleasure in shooting, and when he was satisfied with his own skill, he laughed merrily in self-applause. The young orang meanwhile had been watching his friend's sport from the top of his tree. After a little time, wishing to take part in it, he came down from his observatory and went up to Edward. He looked humble, almost supplicating; evidently he wished to obtain pardon for his past faults. But Edward pouted; he would not turn round, and went on shooting his arrows against the trunk of a tree, without seeming to bestow a thought on the penitent offender. The latter, vexed, tried to seize the bow; Edward pushed him away roughly. The young orang began to cry and bemoan himself, stamping with his foot and rolling on the ground, like a naughty child.

At that moment, the kind of noise that we have already mentioned, and which seemed to be the usual voice of the orangs, was heard from the interior of one of the huts. It was the father or mother of the young orang complaining of the harshness with which their son was treated. Whether the sound was a threat of which poor Edward knew the meaning, or whether he thought he had punished his companion's tricks enough, he turned towards him, smiling. Immediately the young orang uttered a cry of joy, threw himself into his arms, and kissed him on his hands and chest, with transports of affection that no words can describe.

Peace being made, Edward consented at last to give up the bow in question; but his friend used it clumsily, shooting almost at random, and none of his arrows reached the mark.

Furious at his own awkwardness, he threw away the bow, which Edward picked up again, laughing at him. By way of retaliation, the young orang picked up some pebbles from the bed of the stream, and threw them with vigour and dexterity against the trunk of the tree that served for a target. As often as Edward hit the mark with his arrows, so often the orang hit it with his stones, and this equal success excited their pride and pleasure to the highest pitch.

Palmer, crouching down behind a clump of small trees, noticed this scene with mingled curiosity and emotion. His son, then, had some pleasures even in this captivity in which the relations of the human race to that of the brute were so singularly reversed. He could not sufficiently admire the grace and suppleness of this wild youth. Edward's body, strengthened by exercise and open air, presented the finest proportions, and his hair floating about his shoulders gave him a noble appearance. When the youth, with one leg drawn back, in a posture full of natural dignity, held out his bow and prepared to let fly an arrow, he was as beautiful as a Greek Apollo, and this beauty was rendered still more striking by its contrast with his companion's ugliness.

The latter, though his face was expressive of gaiety, and a certain intelligence, though every movement displayed superior strength and agility, presented by the side of this remarkable specimen of the human race every sign of a brute nature.

His prominent jaws, his flat nose, his long hairy arms, his thin legs, reminded one that, in spite of the affection that seemed to exist between him and Edward, in spite of the apparent similarity of their tastes and actions, there was a distance between them as great as that which exists between heaven and earth.

However, the two friends got tired at last of these amusements, and a hoarse call from one of the huts seemed to warn them that it was time to go to rest. Edward, taking his bow and arrows, went towards his hut. The young orang seemed disposed at first to follow him, but another call, more authoritative than the first, induced him at last to obey. He appeared to leave his dear Edward with the greatest reluctance; he overwhelmed him with caresses, and it was only after he had seen him enter his cabin that he climbed the tree to which his mother was calling him.

The time was a favourable one. Edward, being tired, would no doubt go to sleep; it would be easy to surprise him in his sleep. Besides, the orangs scattered about the trees and in the huts seemed themselves to be overpowered with the heat, and would probably relax their usual vigilance. So the planter, set free from the kind of fascination that the presence of his son had exercised over him till then, hastened to beat a retreat, and had the good fortune to succeed in doing so without attracting the enemy's attention.

A few minutes later and he was among his people again.

Deursen, as we have said above, had been directed to lead the Lascars to the other side of the glade frequented by the orangs in such a way as to cut off their retreat into the forest; while Palmer, with the Malays, was to approach the colony in front, and they now set themselves to execute these different movements. They walked in the greatest silence; all conversation, even in a low voice, was forbidden. They were to remain, as much as possible, under the shelter of the trees, and where there were no trees, to crawl on their hands and knees through the long grass. These good arrangements had the happiest results; Palmer and those who accompanied him arrived without any hindrance in sight of the glade, and almost at the same time the cry of a heron, perfectly imitated by one of the Lascars, assured them that Deursen and his people had also reached their appointed post.

Palmer then put his horn to his lips and blew softly a few notes; this was the signal for the two bands to spread themselves out and form a circle round the glade. This movement was executed with extreme precision. Two curved lines were formed, then lengthened out, and then the ends united. There was not more than a space of ten paces between each of the men composing this chain, and nothing that was enclosed within this circle could possibly escape except by flying through the air.

Palmer and Darius held themselves ready to fir ; Van Stetten, whom they had also armed with an enormous gun, seemed very ill at ease. Nothing, however, seemed to justify this uneasiness. The orangs did not show themselves, and if Palmer had not seen a rather numerous band of them a few minutes before with his own eyes, he would have thought that they had deserted the spot.

However, he knew how deceitful this appearance was, and the sudden disappearance of the dangerous adversaries seemed to him the worst possible sign. He would have preferred an open attack on their part to this treacherous silence and stillness. His anxious forebodings were not long in being realized. A dull heavy blow was heard, and a Malay fell as if struck by a thunderbolt. At the same instant, one of those standing nearest to the victim raised his gun to his shoulder, and aimed at the terrible club-bearer in the tree that had struck the blow, but Palmer hastened to interfere.

"Don't shoot! don't shoot!" he said energetically, "or all is lost!" The order was obeyed, and the hunter, muttering angrily, lowered his gun. They raised the unfortunate Malay, but help was in vain; the skull was shattered, and death had been instantaneous.

Palmer had hardly recovered from the horror produced by this occurrence, when the same dull sound, followed immediately by a fall, was heard; this time it was among the Lascars; another man had fallen under the invisible clubs. But this time the planter could not prevent vengeance being taken. The Lascar had hardly measured his length on the ground than a shot was fired, no doubt by one of the friends of the deceased.

It did not appear that the ball could have reached the orangs; but the sound of firing, the first perhaps that had ever echoed through that part of the wood, produced an extraordinary effect. The silence and stillness that had reigned till then among the foliage was suddenly broken. Strange cries rose on all sides; a frightful tumult followed in the trees. The largest branches were snapped asunder as by a tempest, and fell down with a crash at the hunters' feet; little branches, leaves, and parasite plants fluttered about in every direction. At the same time gigantic creatures were seen climbing rapidly to the tops of the highest bombax and pine-trees; they might have been taken for gigantic birds flying with the utmost speed towards the glowing sky.

A few shots were fired again, in spite of Palmer's prohibition, and in spite of the evident impossibility of reaching their agile adversaries; then followed the most perfect silence. No doubt the orangs, safe in their aerial refuges, were again on the watch, and were waiting to see what the next proceedings of their assailants would be.

"Now, now!" cried Palmer, "don't lose a minute—Edward is still in his hut, I know,—I am sure of it. Let us make haste."

He ran towards the hut with Darius and the doctor. As they drew near Edward's miserable cabin, they were rejoined by Deursen, and the negro who acted as his servant. Deursen was about to give Palmer his account of the last occurrences, but the latter had only time to say hastily:

"He is there; stay here."

When they reached the hut they perceived that its inhabitant had closed the entrance with branches; at that very moment he was in the act of piling up the moss and dry leaves that served him for a bed behind the slight enclosure. He appeared dreadfully frightened and much agitated, and overwhelmed with terror, and they could distinctly hear the sound of his oppressed breathing.

What was to be done? Certainly a single blow of a hatchet would suffice to open a breach in the frail building; but that perhaps might drive the young savage to do something blind and desperate. Palmer gave a sign to those, around him to keep silence; then he leaned towards the wall of the hut, and said in a gentle voice, and in English:

"Edward, my boy, don't be frightened; it is I,—it's your father,—I have found you at last, after looking so long for you. I love you still, and I have come to deliver you from the bondage of the orangs."

He was silent and listened; the convulsive movements inside the hut had ceased. Perhaps Edward remembered that he had heard such sounds a few days before; perhaps even his memory went further back, and he tried to recognise the accents of that dear voice, which, without his knowing why, caused him such great agitation. However, his calmness did not last long, he soon became more violently agitated, and his breathing became more laboured.

Palmer continued, in an anxious tender tone:

"My son!—my Edward!—my child!"

Ah, with what a tone was this uttered! The effect of this appeal was prompt and decisive.

"Papa!" cried a trembling voice.

At the same instant the branches were dashed away impetuously, and Edward, pale, his hair dishevelled, and his look wild, darted out of the hut. He did not seem to know what he was about, and he had his bow and arrows in his hand. Trembling all over, and with a strange wild look, his very terror, astonishment, and joy, added to the nobleness of his appearance. When he came into the glade, he stopped, let fly an arrow at random, as if at some invisible object. The arrow fell without any force, a few paces off. Then the poor boy let the bow itself drop from his trembling hands, and looked around him.

A thousand different feelings were depicted on his sunburnt face, at the sight of the persons who stood motionless and silent at the side of the hut; however, the dominant impression seemed to be that of fear. As he tottered, Palmer was on the point of stepping forward to support him; but Edward made a sudden movement as if he were about to run away, and the poor father did not dare to stir from his place.

"Good-morning, Edward," he said gently.

The young savage tried to pronounce a few words, but his speech was confused; he could only make indistinct sounds, and stopped as if ashamed of his weakness.

Nevertheless, these signs of the near a wakening of his enfeebled intellect inspired Edward's friends with the greatest joy. The planter then added:

"My child, won't you kiss your father, who loves you better than anybody? Have you forgotten your father?"

"Father," echoed Edward, with some difficulty.

But he added almost directly, of his own accord and with great clearness:

"Mamma!" This sacred name, the first that rises to the lips of the child, the last that makes the heart of the old man beat,—this name uttered by the young savage, touched those present most deeply. Every eye filled with tears.

"Your mother, poor child," said Palmer, "you will never see again."

But overcoming his emotion, he added:

"You have your father and your cousin Anna, and relations and friends, who will make you forget all your past sufferings."

Edward listened attentively, and seemed to have some difficulty in understanding the meaning of the words addressed to him. He stammered out:

"Father—mother—Anna."

"Ah! he remembers everybody that used to love him," cried Palmer with ecstasy; "and his love returns at the same time as his memory. Already he seems to want to speak, and in a few days—God be praised! my child is given back to me at last."

Till now they had formed a circle round Edward, but without daring to approach him, for it seemed that the least touch would make him rebel. Palmer, after having allowed his son time to get used to the sight of men, spoke a word aside to Darius, who at once gave him a little parcel; he drew out of it one of those blue cotton cloths worn by Hindoos and negroes. It was a very simple garment, but they could not expect at first to impose a more complicated dress on this child of the woods, so impatient of restraint.

Palmer even thought that he must be very careful how he persuaded the youth to let himself be dressed. He first showed him this blue cloth, and made him understand that it was meant for him; then he went gently up to him, and tried to clothe him with the loose drapery. Edward, in spite of his astonishment, trembled directly he was touched, and his muscles became rigid. Happily, a few kind words and signs of affection calmed him. His toilet completed, and it did not take long, he seemed to look at himself with complacency, and burst out laughing with all the naiveté of a child.

Till now the orangs had granted some respite to the band of hunters; but they might change their minds, and the hunters, under these thick trees, were still exposed to their blows. It was not prudent, then, to wait any longer in this place. Besides, Edward, thanks to the caution with which they had acted, seemed to have become sufficiently tame to follow his father and friends without resistance. So Palmer, taking him by the hand, said to him kindly:

"Come, Edward; come, my boy. We must go."

As the young savage let himself be led away, sharp cries were heard from a neighbouring tree; they seemed to express at once sorrow and anger. Edward stopped, and his father, in spite of his efforts, felt him become firm as a rock, while he looked about to see the cause of the noise.

It was the young orang, who had just come out of his hut, and who, seeing the usual companion of his games going away with these unknown invaders, gave himself up to the most violent despair. Bending down from a branch, he gesticulated in a most lively fashion, and brandished a club in a threatening manner. Edward, no doubt, had a real affection for this creature, the only one that loved him in his miserable condition. So he seemed greatly affected by this appeal, and, do or say what they could, he refused to advance. He even stretched out his arms towards the young orang, and answered him with a guttural exclamation. Immediately all the orangs scattered about in the trees uttered their usual growl; then hastily breaking off thick branches from the trees, they threw them with much vigour and skill at the hunters, while the young one redoubled his furious gestures and brandished his club.

"We must not hesitate," said the planter to Darius, "since he will not walk we must carry him; if he resist, we must bind him. God forgive me the violence which I must exercise towards the son for whom I would sacrifice my life! But the orangs seem to intend to attack us in a body, and if they do really attack us, no one knows what will happen. Darius, do what we agreed on."

The negro, unfastening a cord that he wore as a sort of girdle, twisted it quickly round Edward's limbs. The latter, taken up with his companion, never dreamt of the possibility of this violent treatment; and trying to execute one of his impetuous movements, he fell, and would have hurt himself if his father, who was holding him by the arm, had not broken his fall. Nevertheless, neither Palmer nor Darius had counted on his extraordinary strength; hardly had he fallen to the ground than he began to struggle violently. The two men alone could not control his struggles; Deursen, the other negro, and Dr. Van Stetten himself, were obliged to help in reducing him to such a condition that he should have no power to resist. He was soon strongly bound and made completely powerless.

Then he began to utter cries so frightful, so different from the sounds that terror or anger sometimes wring from human beings, that those who heard them never forgot them. He rolled on the ground in a perfect frenzy, biting everything within his reach.

Palmer, greatly agitated, called all the hunters round him; for it was no longer necessary to guard their post now that the object of the expedition was attained. He ordered four of the Malays to lift up Edward, while some of the others carried away the two men killed by the orangs.

"Let us go," he said, "let us go; we must make haste to get out of this thicket. As soon as we reach the plain we shall have nothing more to fear, I hope. Till then—" He had no time to finish his sentence. As the men appointed for the task were going to raise Edward in their arms, the young orang made a prodigious leap from his tree, and raising his club, rushed on the men who he thought were persecuting his friend. His attack was so sudden and so impetuous that the Malays, in self-defence, were obliged to drop their burden on the grass; but the formidable animal was already upon them. As one of them seized his gun, a blow from the club broke his arm a little below the elbow. The orang, howling and leaping, was preparing to strike again, when a shot, fired close to him by a Lascar, entered his breast. The wound was mortal, and streams of dark blood flowed from it. However the quadruman hardly seemed to notice it, and lost none of his indomitable vigour. He threw down his club; and employing no other weapons than his large hands and long muscular arms, he dashed aside the strong men who were guarding Edward without any apparent effort, and threw them roughly to a distance. Then leaning over his friend, he took him in his arms, covered him with kisses, and tried to carry him away to the huts. But then it became evident that his strength was not equal to his courage; twice he raised Edward, twice he let him fall again. They both continued to utter piercing cries, and shed abundant tears; and while the orang tried to set his old companion free, the latter rolled about convulsively on the grass, trying by sudden jerks to break his cords. However, the men who had been so rudely repulsed were on their feet again, and were running to avenge the insult, with the help of the rest of the band. The young orang, in the midst of so many enemies, drew himself up proudly, and tried again to defend Edward, who was unable to defend himself. He had picked up his club, and was brandishing it with spirit, threatening with certain death whoever dared to approach. His enemies never thought of shooting at him again; either they were afraid of hurting each other in the confusion, or perhaps they were filled with pity at sight of the poor creature's devotion to young Palmer. But Elephant-Slayer was not a man to allow himself to be stopped by such scruples. So, while the orang was facing his other assailants, he glided treacherously behind him and buried his *kris* up to the hilt between his shoulders. The young orang turned round quickly. Seizing the bloody blade, he broke it like glass, while with the other hand he aimed a blow with his club at Elephant-Slayer, who avoided it adroitly. The quadruman was on the point of returning to the charge, but he was attacked on all sides at once with *krises*, swords, and bayonets, and he could not defend himself with his club from so many formidable weapons. He was wounded again severely in several places, and yet he did not fall; still standing, with flaming eyes, he would not abandon his captive companion.

The poor creature soon changed his attitude; overpowered by numbers, covered with blood, he threw down his weapon, and ceased all resistance. By his cries, tears, and supplicating gestures, he seemed to be imploring his enemies to have pity on him. His dying look was strangely intelligent. He placed his hands on his gaping wounds; he uttered groans so sad, so expressive, that no human language could equal them. All the spectators of this miserable scene were deeply touched, and Palmer turned away his head with horror. One of the Lascars, perhaps with the intention of putting an end to the sufferings of Edward's defender, gave him a blow with a bayonet; but he had miscalculated the strength that the orang still possessed, for the latter, seizing the weapon, broke it as he had broken the *kris*, while his dying look seemed to reproach the assailant for this piece of unnecessary cruelty.

This frightful struggle was drawing to its close, when someone cried out:

"Look out! The other orangs are upon us."

Every eye was turned to the spot indicated. The man who had given the alarm had exaggerated a little; the greater number of the orangs, posted on the tops of the trees, were content with making a furious noise; two alone were running towards the hunters, with the evident intention of attacking them; they were the father and mother of the young orang.

They could be seen leaping from tree to tree, breaking off in their anger the tops of the palm-trees, and scattering around them a cloud of leaves, moss, and parasitic plants. If a single orang of less than full growth had sufficed to keep the whole band in check, what might not be feared from these two terrible animals, of frightful size and strength, and excited by the cries of their young one in distress?

Palmer perceived the greatness of the danger.

"Keep close round us," he cried, "and let us get out of this detestable thicket as fast as possible."

He took his son in his arms himself, and carried him off in spite of the cries and feeble resistance that Edward (being so securely bound) could still make.

The wounded orang was clinging to his friend's leg, and allowed himself to be dragged along for a minute without letting go his hold; but his wounds had exhausted his strength, and he was obliged to give in, uttering a last sad cry as he did so.

The hunters, to whom their chief's command had been transmitted in different languages, hastened to gather round the principal group, and the retreat was hastily commenced. Then the two orangs dropped to the ground and ran to their dying young one. Happily, being completely taken up with his sufferings, they never thought of troubling themselves about the hunters, who, if they had, would have found some difficulty in making their escape through the trees.

The mother took her young one in her arms; she examined his wounds, kissed them, tried to stanch the blood, and shed many tears over him, while the father brandished his club and growled.

In a little time the rest of the orangs, being called by the afflicted family, ran to them, and seemed to share their grief and anger.

The young orang had just expired as the band of hunters lost sight of them, and the others, according to the usual custom of their race, covered his body with leaves and branches. His mother rolled about on the grass, and filled the forest with her lamentations.

CHAPTER XXIII

A little later the band of hunters halted under a clump of trees, which were so completely isolated that there was no fear of their being surprised by the orangs. This rest was much needed, for the heat, after so much excitement and fatigue, was overpowering. Besides, they had to bury the men who had been killed by the terrible apes, and a grave at the foot of a palm-tree was quickly dug.

Palmer, in spite of the lives that Edward's deliverance had cost, could not conceal his joy, and he gazed with much affection at the son whom his perseverance and courage had saved.

"Now, Mr. Palmer," said the Governor, "we are surely free at last from orangs. They seem to understand that it is dangerous to be within our reach."

"We must not be too confident," answered Palmer thoughtfully; "I know facts about these strange animals that make one almost doubt if there be not a sort of diabolical intelligence in their malice. I wish we were on the other side of the lake. Let us hurry on."

When they reached the edge of the marsh, the sun was beginning to go down, and the heat had decidedly abated; nevertheless, the volcanic blocks of stone, forming the ridge, were still so burning hot that the Lascars could not walk over them with their naked feet without considerable pain.

Edward, who had become tractable again, walked quietly between the two men who were appointed specially to watch over his movements. Palmer, perceiving that the young savage, dressed in nothing but a blue cotton cloth, had his bare skin exposed to the rays of the still scorching sun, went to the baggage and took out a piece of calico, and threw it over Edward's shoulders. On first feeling the light stuff, Edward tried to throw it off, but very soon the comfort it afforded made him change his mind. He left off twisting himself about, and looked round to see to whom he was indebted for this relief. Then his countenance lighted up, and he said in a voice that retained all his old childish tones:

"Papa! papa!"

Nothing could express Palmer's delight at this entirely spontaneous proof of filial affection.

"Ah, now he knows me!" he cried proudly. "Yes, he knows me quite well, in spite of my long beard and gray hair!"

"Papa!—mamma!—Anna!" repeated the youth.

Palmer felt strongly tempted to press him in his arms, but was afraid to do so too soon, for fear of frightening him away.

"Come!" he exclaimed, "it won't be so difficult or take so long to teach him as we might have feared. Edward," he added, addressing his son, "Anna will be your teacher, your companion, and your constant friend again, as she used to be: she promised me she would."

Edward seemed to understand the words spoken to him more and more easily. He laughed, clapped his hands, and repeated the names of his father, mother, and Anna. However, in the midst of his gaiety he appeared suddenly to remember something, and pointing towards the part of the wood they had just quitted, said in a frightened tone:

"Orangs!"

"You need not be afraid of those savage beasts any more," replied the planter; "there are a great number of us, and we are well armed; we shall be able to defend you. By-and-by you shall tell us all you have suffered among them—what privations and pains you endured before you got used to that miserable way of living. But now you can be easy. You are under the protection of your father and friends."

In spite of these assurances, Edward still seemed to feel some vague uneasiness at times, and he looked behind him frequently with an expression of alarm and grief.

However, they had now reached the edge of the lake. There they found some tall, leafy trees, and some shade; which was a great relief to them after their long journey in the sun.

The hunters began to cross the ridge of rocks, and Palmer made all the men pass on in line before he did. Accompanied by a Lascar, he was preparing to follow them, when among the leaves of an enormous pandanus-tree at the edge of the water he thought he saw something move; a thought struck him:

"Can it be Edward's captor pursuing him?" he murmured.

He had his hatchet as well as his gun. He walked resolutely towards the tree, and the Lascar was courageous enough to go with him. Palmer did not stop till he came within two steps of the tree, and still watched the thick foliage carefully. There was certainly an orang that had taken up his station in the lower branches, and was now brandishing his club and gnashing his teeth. It was of the largest size and tremendously strong. The planter recognised Edward's captor at the first glance.

"Accursed brute!" he exclaimed, "it is to you I am indebted for all the greatest troubles of my life. Now for it!" The savage animal was coming down, growling and brandishing his club, but Palmer did not stir, and planted his foot firmly, hatchet in hand.

"Take care," cried the Lascar, "the orang is just upon you; he is going to—"

"So much the better!" said Palmer. "Leave him to me."

The Lascar, in spite of this order, took advantage of the moment the orang showed himself to fire at him, but the quadruman did not seem to notice the wound. Hanging to a branch by one of his hind hands, he let his great body fall forwards, while with one of his fore hands he swung round a club as thick as a man's thigh. The momentum, increased by the whole weight of the orang, was so great that the very air hissed, and the club, striking the trunk of the pandanus, made the bark fly off in strips. But Palmer, as quick as thought, had sprung on one side, and taking advantage of the moment when his enemy was himself stunned with the violence of the shock, he struck him a blow with his hatchet that sounded as if the blade had met with a block of granite. The blow clove the skull of the formidable animal, yet he did not let go at once, and remained hanging, wildly swinging his club. Palmer, with inexorable coolness, dealt him another blow, no less violent than the first. This time the stroke was mortal; he fell, palpitating still and still holding his weapon, on the grass, which was already bathed in his blood.

"Dead at last!" cried Palmer triumphantly; "I have nothing more to fear for my son." And he rejoined the other hunters in all haste.

They followed the same path till the evening, and it was far into the night when they reached the house, where Mrs. Surrey had prepared refreshments for all the hunters.

We have no need to describe the delight of Anna and her mother. Palmer rewarded the Malays and Lascars liberally.

Edward's education had to be begun again, but it proved a great success, thanks especially to the intelligent and loving pains that the gentle Anna bestowed upon him.

Some years later the marriage of Edward and Anna crowned the hopes of these youthful companions and of their devoted father, who would have thought himself the happiest of men if only his dear Elizabeth had lived to share his joy.

THE END

ABOUT THE AUTHOR

Élie Berthet (1818-1891) was a 19th century French novelist. His works include *L'enfant des bois* (1865) (as *The Wild Man of the Woods*, 1868), and *The Pre-Historic World* (1876; translated into English by Mary J. Safford in 1879) and *La Bête du Gévaudan* (1858), a novel about a famous feral child.